EL NIÑO

To Nill C,

Mick Donnellan

26/02/12.

Mick Donnellan

ORIGINAL WRITING

© 2012 Mick Donnellan
Cover photos by Eibhlin Heard, Tom Page and Rick Adams
Chief Editor Imelda Heaphy

ISBN: 978-1-908817-54-9

A CIP catalogue for this book is available from the National Library.

Published by Original Writing Ltd., Dublin, 2012.

Printed by Clondalkin Group, Clonshaugh, Dublin 17

For my twin brother, Seamus.

Taken, yet always here.

They did not know that a new life is not given for nothing; that it has to be paid dearly for, and only acquired by much patience and suffering, and great future efforts.

Fyodor Dostoyevsky, *Crime and Punishment.*

CHAPTER I

Her name was El Niño. Her father called her that because the night she was born there was a storm. He said it signified the way she was to live her life. I met her in an elevator. Wanted to go three floors and forget about it. Instead, everything changed.

Thing is, bout meeting a girl like her, it hits you like a curve ball. It's not like you get written notice. It's fast, short, and leaves you spinning. I hit floor three and asked: 'Goin up?'

She purred. 'Third floor.'

'Arts?'

'Yeah.'

It was the last day of the semester and I'd spent it following a lecturer around. His wallet bulged so big, I coulda jumped up right there in the class and taken him out. But that's the downfall. That's how mosta my friends spend their holidays in a cage. They get impatient, can't wait, always want the big scoop.

The guy taught socialism. Preached about a perfect world, one without money. I disagreed. What a fuckin hypocrite. I looked down and saw this wad popping out, thought: fuck, I gotta get me a piece of that. We all like some extra grade. But I waited. Scoped him out. Asked him a question after, like: 'Excuse me, Mr. McKenna? But where can I get a copy of *The Communist* Manifesto?'

He looked me up and down, said: 'Call up to my office this afternoon. I'll have one there, costs €3.50. That alright?'

Thought: fuck you, selling the goddamn pamphlet that says we should kill the capitalist. Makes me sick. He bent to get his briefcase and I saw my chance. Went ahead and some chick came from behind.

'Sorry, Mr. McKenna? Do you have a minute?'

Ah, fuck off hippy kids, always want the revolution. Nearly had him too. Heart beating fast, going in for the kill and snared.

Bitch didn't even know what the fuck she was talking about, just trying to sound all smart and shit.

Left. Thought: get him later, maybe at the office, send him somewhere.

Started the game bout ten years ago. Only been caught once. Old man clocked me hitting some geyser on his way from the post-office. Pension hanging out. Was in fast, hit hard. Knocked him, played the Good Samaritan. Pulled him up with one hand, took his cash with the other. Next thing I see is sky. Father staring down, frothing. 'Give it back,' he says, 'ya thief. Never been no stealin in this family til now, and I'll knock it outta ya.'

He had a heart attack six months later. Tough times. Needed to bring home some grade. Took up robbing again. Probably turn in his grave, but, what're ya gonna do? Get a fuckin job?

The elevator passed the first floor. I took in her intoxicating perfume. It smelled like confidence, prowess, intrigue, desire. Asked: 'English?'

'Classics and Soc&Pol. You?'

'English and Soc&Pol. Goin go see McKenna, bout buyin The Manifesto.'

'Were you there today?'

'Yeah. Bullshit.'

'I thought it was interesting.'

'Whatever you're into.'

Second floor. She scanned me from the toes up, blinked and asked: 'Why you want The Manifesto then?'

Thought fast. 'Take a read over the summer, give it a chance, see if this Marx kat's really got anythin to say.'

'What about the revolution?'

'Fuck the revolution. I wasn't around.'

'Have you taken this up with McKenna?'

'No. And the bastard wants €3.50. Tells me he wants a revolt against the capitalist, but I gotta pay for it – fuck that.'

She raised her eyebrows. Style and attitude. 'Maybe it's all about progress.'

'Or a lost cause.'

'Or the bigger picture?'

'Or floor three. Beauty before the beast, babe.'

'Interesting ride.'

'Went too fast. Gimme your number and we'll take it up later.'

'You don't waste time.'

I shrugged. It felt the right thing to do. Silence threatened.

She scribbled it out and said: 'I'll let you buy me a drink, see how it works from there.'

'I'm honoured.'

'Name's El Niño.'

'El Niño?'

'There was a storm on the night I was born; my father said it signified the way I was to live my life.'

'I'm Charlie, after my father, and my grandfather, and his old man too. One long line of Charlie.'

She smiled a hundred suns. 'Cute. See you this evening.'

Walked, with the feel of her wallet inside my coat. Silly bitch. Wrote the number, left her bag open. What was I supposed to do? Sorry Mr. Opportunity, no one round, call back later?

Got to his office. He was bald with a gut. Sat typing something, probably more overpriced communism. Knocked, said: 'Mr. McKenna? I talked to you today, after your lecture, about buyin *The Communist Manifesto?*'

Turned, fixed his glasses, scrutinised. Obvious disdain. Must have been the clothes — leather jacket and cap on backwards. 'Yes, yes, Marxist Economics, wasn't it?'

'Yeah.'

I looked around. Saw books on Orwell, Nietzsche, Smith, Rawls, Hobbes, Locke, Rousseau, the whole fuckin crew. Irony apparent. He ruffled in his desk, took out a copy, said: 'Well, Mr...'

'Charlie.'

'Well Charlie, that's €3.50, please.'

Took out my stash, asked: 'You got change for a hundred?'

He frowned. I saw the disappointment. The dilemma being: the profit or the cause? Checks his pockets, looks around. 'I... let me see, I...don't...at the moment. Anything smaller?'

'Nope.'

'Oh.'

Frown time for me. 'Oh?'

'Tell you what, you can call back with…no, actually, hang on and I'll see if Doris is in the office…she might have some.'

Disco. Took his fat ass up and waddled out. Almost caused a tremor on the corridor. This place is a real fuckin Jurassic Park. Looked around, wallet on the table. Could be obvious. Fuck it, not here for the socialism. Acted fast, skimmed the notes, left a few. Didn't want him seeing the wad all thin. These guys looked after nothing better than dust. Heard him thank Doris. Probably fuckin her, blowjob at lunch and a cash bonus on the side. Some revolution.

He returned with: 'Yes, got some change from Doris. A hundred you say?'

'Aye, captain.'

Did the exchange. The cold greasy feel of money changing paws. The fear that someone's gonna snap the goods and screw the whole deal. Could get ugly. Everyone just stay cool. I took the pamphlet. Watched him, like a starved dog, stuff the money into a sweaty pocket. He didn't open the wallet. Wouldn't be like a man of *the cause*. Watched his beard and smile. Yellow teeth. Stink of cigars and wet armpits. No exercise. Always takes the lift. The stress. Thought: arteries. Could see the cholesterol, like a ghost's aroma, hovering around his head. The red patch at top, screaming with rage, like follicles pulled with pliers. He stood salivating, jingling coins, asked: 'You like it?'

'Oh yeah. Can't wait to get a read of this. I've been after it for a while now. I love Marx. He's my hero.'

He turned his back, walked to the table, dismissed me with: 'Enjoy…'

Left and took the lift back down. Could still sense El Niño. Her scent vamoosed from the mirror behind. In my head, an image of McKenna sitting in his office, with a smile for another one recruited to his illusions. And behind him, an ugly sceptre, hanging with menace, waiting to sever his spine. And the wallet lying open, gutted like a slaughtered animal. At least he got €3.50 back. Threw the pamphlet in the bin and walked home.

She looked beautiful in the photograph. Sallow, and those hazel eyes that tell you she understands almost everything, like they can see into your soul. She had the usual: cards, a licence and some receipts. Some looked sentimental, others just there. There was change and a few notes. Counted hers and the communist's money. Made the day handsome.

Sat back and my bed creaked. Outside, it was still bright as the church bells rang for six. Took out her number, tempted to call. Monday was a bad night on the street. No crowd, no anonymity; no action. Need: patience and tact. I picked up her wallet and put it in an envelope. Still sticking by the code. It's an honour thing, but it's a karma thing too. Always have to post the wallet back. Every time. Get the money and send home the rest. Just coz. Keeps us in business. Poor fools fill it up again so the next guy can hit 'em.

An hour of bored contemplation passed. Then. She sounded weird on the phone. Her voice all broken and soft.

'Hey, storm girl, you wanna get that drink?'

'Sorry, Pablo, broke like a train wreck.'

'No way, kitten, how you gonna cause a hurricane at home?'

'No dust, honey. No choice.'

'Lose it on a pony?'

'It was stolen.'

'Stolen?'

She let the word linger. I was getting pissed off. Just wanted outta the house. Wasn't in the game for the guilt trip. Said: 'Guys like that should be fuckin castrated. A girl like you, mindin your own wax...'

'Done and dusted now. Point is, no grade.'

'Negative.'

'Don't get ya.'

'I'm good for it.'

'No way.'

'Way.'

She laughed and said: 'Forget it.'

'What ya gonna do?'

'Sit at home.'

'Like a Toblerone?'

'Spose so.'

'No go tornado. I'm supposed to buy anyway. Massimo's at eight.'

She let it dance, then said: 'Massimo's at eight? Hope you're flush.'

'Roger that.'

'Rendezvous at eight then.'

Click.

We were both early. The place had a Spanish edge. Salsa vibe. Red wine. Candles on the tables. Smell of varnish. She sensed me come in and looked up. Those eyes: searching, intelligent and deep. It was seven forty-five. She was in a long black jumper and tight blue jeans. I asked: 'Pint?'

'Vodka and coke.'

'Comin up. Cubes?'

'No thanks. I'm cool enough.'

Drank them. Got more. She said: 'So hit me with a life secret.'

'Where do I start?'

'Why're you drinking Cidona?'

'I was an alcoholic at sixteen.'

'That the last time you drank?'

'Seventeen. Bout five years ago.'

'Must've started young.'

'Fourteen. Bushes, car parks, football pitches, all scattered with flagons of cider.'

'Just cider?'

'Everythin. Name the poison.'

'Sounds wild.'

'Or tragic.'

'That too.'

The clatter of a pub getting busy. Stools. Glasses. Music. Atmosphere. The beermats on the table soaked in lager temptation. I went on. 'Guy told me once; he was in a pub in my hometown, place called Ballinrobe, met one of the locals from the old days. Local says: "Where's Charlie these days? I never see him." and my guy replies: "He lives in Galway now. He doesn't drink anymore." and the local, all fulla surprise says: "Jaysus, and he was good at it too."'

We sipped. She raised an eyebrow, asked: 'When did you hit rock bottom?'

'Floored a cop.'

'Do any time?'

'No. Close, but was lucky with the judge. Your turn.'

'Before college, I travelled for a year.'

'Oz?'

'Thailand, Beijing, Australia. Some of Europe.'

'Favourite place?'

'Prague.'

'Why?'

'It's beautiful. I'd love to go back.'

'Why don't ya?'

'Debts.'

'Oh. Another twist?'

'Yeah, go then. I'm enjoying myself.'

Felt the first wrench of guilt. Detrimental. Thought: what the fuck am I doing? Shot it down. At the bar, got her the drink. It took a while. Enough time to contemplate the top shelf. Vodka ghosts and wild cider demons. Paid and sat back down. Stayed there til close. Chewing the fat, shooting the breeze, give it a name, call it talking. Bouncer came over, high on power, clapped and said: 'Come on, guys, love is portable.'

Drained the chalice and left.

Exterior. Front of the pub. Night.

I asked: 'Your place or mine?'

'Where you live?'

'Forster Court.'

'Fuck that.'

'You?'

'Laurel Park.'

'Sounds good. We get a cab?'

She was kinda drunk, said: 'Let's walk. I need the air.'

Came down by Monroe's and walked up passed the canal behind The Roisín Dubh. Lit a smoke and watched her. Conflicted about business and pleasure. Then, fuck it. Why not? I was sending her the wallet back and gave her all the dollars in vodka. Odds and evens. It's all good. Got to the old playground, with the graffiti on the wall. She saw the swings, said: 'I wanna swing.'

'Eh?'

'Swings, come on.'

'Forget it.'

'C'mon, I love the playground....'

She tried to walk then tripped on the path. No reflexes. Thud. Then laughter. She stayed down, looking at the sky, said: 'Come lie with me.'

Lay back; put my head on her shoulder. Staring at the stars. A light wind, a cold whisper, almost gentle. She said: 'This is a good night.'

'Oh yeah.' I dragged hard, blew some crystals. 'I stole your wallet today.'

'I know.'

'You know? Then what's with the catatonia?'

'I knew you'd call. This way I get free booze and my money back.'

Finished the cigarette and walked to her place. Through the college. Loud drunks hanging around outside the church. Shoes hanging on the power lines — sign of a dealer. Walked through Ardilaun Road and came up by Laurel Park. She lived in 49, top of the hill, light in the porch.

Exterior. Front of her house. Late.

She asked: 'Want a nightcap?'

Made it to the stairs. Enter passion. Luscious breasts. Skin, creamy and soft. Kissed her all around; neck tasted like peaches. She took off my shirt and went lower. Got naked and went for glory. It was animal. Hard, rough and fast. Calmed down and went upstairs.

Interior. Bedroom. Large bed. Smell of lavender. Purple walls and a poster of Guevara. Stereo in the corner. Went to a rack of tunes. Saw: Clapton, Oldfield and Moby. Put in the whale, track nine, *Extreme ways*. Greatest tune of all time.

Laid back and took in the beats, she sat on top. Hair tickled my face and her nipples rubbed hard on my chest. Locked legs and went in.

Interior. Vagina. Moist.

It was: smooth and passionate. After, went for Oldfield, *Tubular Bells*. She asked: 'What do you think about death?'

'He's a bastard.'

'Seriously.'

'He's a bastard. Why d'ya ask?'

'How do you want to die?'

'It's not somethin I think about. You?'

'By choice. I don't wanna ever get old. Ever.'

'What, check out on your terms?'

'I don't know. When I think the only way is down, that's when I wanna go. Not hang around passed my sell-by date, all leathery like a dried fruit.'

'Deep.'

'Makes sense.'

'Whatever does it for ya.'

Wrapped in the smell of our juices. Clammy and warm. She said: 'I wanna hit the road again too. See more, do more.'

'But you ain't got the cash.'

'Not yet.'

'Not yet?'

'Folks left me some dough.'

'Where they gone?'

'Died in a car accident.'

'How much they leave?'

'Can't touch it until I'm twenty-one.'

'When's that?'

'Couple of months.'

'And then you're gone?'

'Yeah. Pay the debts, book a flight and party like crazy.'

She paused. Then said: '€50.000, something like that.'

She looked at me. I looked at her. We looked at each other. Then she lay back and lit a cig, said: 'You think I'm crazy.'

'A little.'

'I don't know, it's not that I wanna die, it's that I just wanna do something first, something that says I lived.'

'I don't really think that far ahead.'

'What would you if someone told you tomorrow…if someone told you I was gone….'

'Just met ya kid. Tough call. What d'ya want me to say?'

'I dunno. Something profound.'

I took the smoke from her hand. Dragged heavy; thought, blew a passive cloud, said: 'Think I'd go vodka&redbull and wash it down with a pint of cider. Then chew on some tequila worms.'

'After five years?'

'Yeah, then do the waltz with a bottle of Jack. World needs women like you. If y'all start dyin, then I don't wanna be round neither. No point.'

'But you've just met me.'

'I've seen all I need to see.'

She sat up, put a palm under her chin, said: 'You're a cold fish.'

'I just complimented you.'

'That's not what I mean. You're like…detached.'

'People been tellin me that my whole life.'

Third time was slow, intense and sensual. Saw us through til dawn. The birds were out and the dim light came through the curtain. My lids were heavy. I looked into her brown pupils. Where am I now? She was awake and alert and she stared. I blinked, just like a photograph, and slept.

CHAPTER TWO

In the morning she was gone. Exit El Niño. No goodbye. Got up, put on my threads. Her scent, her spirit, heavy in the bedroom air. Went home. Posted her wallet on the way, money included. Hung out at the house, thought she'd call. No bells.

Later, took a walk to the Spanish Arch. Warm day, summer kicking in. Wanted a read and brought some Banville, *Athena*.

Settled on the steps across from the green. Opened the leaves and looked for my page. Saw the shadow, then heard the question. 'Don't suppose you're lookin for work?'

Looked up and saw a big guy playing a game of clouds, the sun shining down all around him. Answered: 'No, sorry bud. Think you got the wrong guy.'

Looked back at my book, thought he'd take the hint. Wasn't having any. Clapped his hands, real agitated. Scratched his head some more, his shadow dancing on the ground. Thought: junkie; needs a fix, trying to hit the spot with an old friend he never had. Did a mental budget. Would help out if he asked. Big arms too, and a boxer top. Looked for tracks. Negative. Could be on Ice. Something like that. He continued with: 'You grew up with a guy called Kramer.'

The world took a fuckin speed wobble, felt like someone had put a can of cider in a sock and hit me across the jaw. Looked up, said: 'Yeah, what's your point?'

'He's my boss.'

Wanted to say: Get the fuck outta my face, asked: 'You serious?'

'You think I'd joke about somethin like that?'

Stayed mute, getting uneasy. Figured that world was in the past, said: 'I don't remember you in any of the old crews.'

He smiled, said: 'Name's P.J.' Extended his hand, continued with: 'Came in soon after you left, heard the whole story. You still workin?'

Shook, said: 'Yeah, but gone solo. I like to take my own falls now.'

'I hear ya.'

He looked into the distance, contemplating, then said: 'Me and a couple of the guys are talkin bout a job over here, if you're interested. We could do with a guy like you in the crew.'

'Makin good grade myself. Don't think I need the risk.'

'Keeps life interestin.'

He was more relaxed now, like we had an affinity — guess we had. I asked: 'Anythin to do with the snow?'

He raised his palms, said: 'Just a normal job, man. That's a different side of the operation.'

I left it a few seconds, went: 'I'll think about it.'

He gave a salute and left a cyclone in his wake. Some hoods waited for him by the water. Tried to read but couldn't concentrate. I watched them from the corner of my eye — P.J pointing me out and telling my history. Heard a quote on a flick once — *'A man can't change what he is.'* I closed the book and went over, said: 'Well, men?'

We all shook and showed respect. A real crowd of Corleones. P.J drank from a flagon of cider. Pushed it my way.

'No thanks, man. I'm still in the desert.'

'Fuck off?'

'Fraid so.'

We shot the shit for a while. Soon there was only three of us left. P.J, a guy called Joe and yours truly. Took out my smokes and offered all around. Cleaned my supply. Sparked and thought: time to get to the point, said: 'Let's get to the point.'

P.J took the stand. 'Chartbusters. Been scopin it for a while. Think we have it down for about forty five large.'

Whistled some toxins, said: 'Where'd you get your stats?'

'Knew a kid, part-timer, caught with his hand in the cookie jar. Got fired. Now he's bitter and wants compo.'

'He on the job?'

'No.'

'Good, coz he sounds fuckin stupid.' They were silent. Didn't like the blunt edge, but, fuck them; we were robbers, not lovers.

This was strictly business. 'Need dates, times, vehicles, stats on security. This ain't no Mickey Mouse shit you're talkin about.'

Instrumental. Then Joe said: 'Hey, Charlie, you got an edge, some style and a history, but how bout a little respect?'

Looked, dragged hard, said: 'Gimme one good fuckin reason and I'll think about it. I ain't goin to prison coz I took a risk with a couple of amateurs....'

P.J. intervened. 'Yeah, we got it down, been on it for months. This is our line of work.'

Took my eyes off Joe, turned and said: 'When?'

'Two weeks.'

Decision time. Lotta cash if it came off. Was depending on a good summer, could be a head start, said: 'I'll be in touch.'

-

Exterior. Night. Shop Street. Days later. She still hadn't called. I took it as a one-night stand. Convinced myself that I didn't care, that she was unhinged, and I needed to stay out of the abyss anyway.

Business was quiet, no whales. Mid-week fluctuated. Sometimes I hit an innocent tour bus, Americans or something, and they ain't no challenge. Other nights I'm stuck with the natives and they got me down. Real shrewd punters. I had an hour in the evening outside Corbett Court. Best place to scope. Folks always coming out counting money. Easy to pick the simple ones. Large coats, big pockets, stuff the wallet down the side and forget about it. Others have bags of clothes, food, shoes, and leave their dust in with the merchandise. Stop at the bus shelter and I'm there.

Hung out around Brown Thomas, just watching. Heart not in it. Leaned against the window and put on some tunes. Checked out the folks waiting for people that were late, sending texts and looking impatient. Should been cold but I was more numb. Thought again about calling her but decided against it. Beat the temptation with thoughts of P.J and the job. Hadn't called him yet either. Maybe tomorrow. Maybe not. The Chemical Brothers played a good riff. Tapped my feet on the ground, palms got wet against the ledge. Figured I should take a step back from the robbing, maybe call it a night.

Walked towards Eyre Square, destination unknown. Taxis flew by; girls in groups and short skirts, all seemed to be blonde. The cops hung around the corner at Holland's shop, chatting but aware. Good move to scale down.

She came past The Imperial and caught me off guard. Hit me on the shoulder and said: 'Hey, Charlie?'

She was looking good. Some guy with her. He was tall, dressed slick, greasy hair. He looked Italian, like someone you'd call Luigi. I felt strong vibes, possessive ones. She was all in black but her eyes were bright and sparkled. Bracelets and beads on her wrists. She took her hair in both hands and tied it in a mock ponytail, chest out. I searched for something smart but nothing came. Took out my smokes, didn't offer, sparked and said: 'Just doin the late shift.'

Luigi looked pissed, like he was in a hurry. He was watching her; anxious to wrap things up. She said: 'I got your parcel in the post.'

'All in order I expect?'

He spoke, real upper class, using all his g's, said: 'We should get going.'

She ignored it with: 'What time you clocking off?'

I took a drag, shrugged and said: 'Windin down now, thinkin of callin it a night. Who's the greaseball?'

'That's not very nice.'

'I don't do nice.'

He spoke again. 'I'm standing right here.'

I took another drag and asked her to translate. She laughed and said: 'It's good to see you.'

Luigi said: 'The queues will be atrocious.' He had one foot ready to leave.

She gave me a wink and grazed my arm lightly with her palm as she left. I walked without looking back. Had mixed emotions. Figured it was the end of what had never really started. Switched the sounds to Killswitch Engaged, *When Darkness*

Falls. Wanted to do something crazy. Had notions of picking up a random chick and fuckin her stupid, just for revenge. Then thought: what do I care? It ain't like we're fuckin married.

And who the fuck says a word like *atrocious*?.

I robbed half the city in retribution. Every kat that looked remotely like Luigi got cleaned. Shoulda been more careful, but I didn't get twigged once. I steered clear of the square and the pigs on patrol. Did The Living Room, Bazaar, Tíg Colí, and Tí na Nóg. All places full of the Pope's children. Accessories left on tables and counters, bags on the floor. Pretended I was a glass collector. They were so busy sending text messages that they wouldn't have noticed a nuclear strike. I even thought about going to Halo and hitting the real money monkeys, but I'd stick out too damn much and I figured she'd be in there anyway.

Night still young. The pubs aroma rode with me. Beer, shots and alcopops. Notions of a once-off bout of self-devastation. Fought it. Thought about an alternative. Go shoot some pool, try and read. Held no appeal. Money was accumulating. Put on some more heavy tracks, willing time to pass. Walked round by the docks. It was dark and quiet. Ships brooding on my left, stench of seaweed. Figured it could be dangerous but deep down I was looking for trouble. Got to Padraigs and the truth hit me. Subconscious playing tricks. House for the shippers, rarely closed. Quiet and personal too, none of the superpub trendy shit. Temptation kicked into overdrive. Heart going, legs weak. Arguments for and against. Getting swayed.

Interior. Pocket. Vibration.

She wanted to meet. I asked: 'What if I say no?'

She played assertive and said: 'Don't be ridiculous.'

'What about Luigi?'

'Who's Luigi?'

'He looks Italian.'

'He's from Gort.'

Pause. 'Where'd ya send him?'

'Does it matter?' She clicked her tongue, asked: 'We hooking up or what?'

'What you wanna do?'

'I got a plan.'

I was walking in an aimless circle, around the cracked footpath and random pieces of age-old gum. Fisherman type came outta the pub and a piece of atmosphere escaped. Trad music and good Guinness.

She asked: 'Where the hell are you anyway?'

'Docks.'

'Thinking bout the dive?'

'Along those lines.'

'Meet me at the Cathedral, near the front entrance.'

'How long you gonna be?'

'Ten minutes.'

'I'll start walkin out.'

Click.

Came round by Brennan's Yard and up through Quay Street. Warm wind. Smell of fast food. Distant sound of breaking glass. Laughing drunk women. The pubs still calling, like a hook in my stomach, tryna reel me in. Saw Luigi outside The Front Door, phone to his ear, looking constipated. The poor cunt.

Came over the Salmon Weir Bridge. Taxi waiting outside the main gate.

Got in.

She was checking her voicemails.

Cabbie asked: 'Where to now?'

She said: 'Laurel Park.'

Got there. She was finished on the blower and powered it down, turned to me and said: 'Be out in a second.'

Clocked the meter. Getting pricey. Cabbie was quiet, robotic. He pulled down the window, sparked a smoke

and said: 'Nice houses them.'

'They're alright, yeah.'

She came out with bags in each arm. Opened the cab and shoved them in beside me. Sat in and told him to face it for Salthill. He threw his smoke out the window and swung a one-eighty.

I checked out the luggage – a bag of drink – vodka, with orange to mix and a few cans of cider. Recipe for destruction.

Got to the prom and she told him to keep going to Silverstrand. Bright streetlight and the night through the window. Traffic quiet, purring engine of the taxi and a smell like leather and stale cigarettes. Got out. She paid and tipped him. I took out the stash and watched the wheels pull away.

Exterior. Silverstrand beach. Summer's night.

She walked to the sand and found a groove by the wall. Then laid out the blanket. I followed her down and she said: 'It's the Summer Solstice, longest day of the year.'

'Looks pretty dark to me.'

'We're gonna watch the sunrise. I've always wanted to do this.'

'Camp on the beach?'

'Yeah.'

'We ain't even got a tent.'

'Who needs one?'

She sat back, opened the vodka and took a long swig. Times gone by I'd've nearly drank the whole bottle in that same motion. I sat beside her and sunk into the sand through the blanket. The stars were out and the night was warm. The stone scraped against my spine until I found a comfortable crevice. I took out the orange and drank from the neck. We watched the ocean with touching shoulders. Bright reflection from the moon on the water. She said: 'So what was with the jealousy buzz?'

'The what?'

I lit a smoke. She kicked off her shoes and crossed her feet on the blanket. I took off my jacket and threw it to the side. 'I'm an intuitive chick, Charlie. You won't fool me.'

'I think I was surprised.'

'At what?'

'Every guy wants to be the first, the only and the last.'

'Bullshit.'

'It's true.'

'And where does that leave women?'

'We don't think about it.'

'You should.'

'It's easier not to.'

'We can't just sit around and fuck one guy our whole lives.'

Had no answer. She swigged and said: 'It's not all about stamina; it's the other stuff too.'

'Like what?'

'You can care about more than one person at the same time.'

'Yeah, but they gotta split you seven different ways?'

'They don't know.'

'They might wanna know.'

'I don't care.'

'I don't buy it.'

'I'm not asking you to.'

'So who's Luigi, then?'

'Material boyfriend. He's got the car, the job, some of the looks and he wants a lady to top it all off.'

'And you do the honours?'

'We hook up and hang out. He pays the way, buys the booze, and introduces me to his friends.'

'He's got *friends*?'

'People like him. Young, rich, competitive. Wannabe tycoons.'

'And you smile and look pretty?'

'Yeah. He buys me jewellery, and other presents too. He's ok.'

'But he thinks you're *his*.'

'No. And I don't feel guilty, either. He knows I'm no angel and I don't ask what he does when I'm not around. No boats rocked, everybody wins.'

She drank some more and looked out over the sea. I had a question, thinking bout how to phrase it when she read my mind.

'You wanna know if I sleep with him at the end of the night.'

'I wanna ask, but I'm not sure if I wanna know.'

'I won't be accountable for things I did before I met you.'

'One step at a time babe. We're still in early days.'

She took a long drink, relished it, said: 'You think I'd be contaminated if you knew another man had me. You're all the fucking same.'

'I won't hold you accountable for anythin, kid. It's not my style, and I got my own demons. Yesterday's history, tomorrow's a mystery.'

'I told ya, I'm not taking death lying down. You wanna talk about morality? Fuck morality.'

'I never said I was jealous, just surprised.'

'Whatever.'

She took another good swirl and left the bottle down hard. Blinked at the ocean. Long eyelashes. The water's lament. Her thoughts in the night. She looked back at me. Those eyes again.

I asked: 'Where do I come into this?'

'The jury's still out on you, Charlie. But don't worry, you're doing good.' She took another drink. Then. 'You nice and head fucked?'

'It's still digestin, but you were right.'

'Bout you being jealous?'

'Yeah.'

'Course I was, why d'ya care anyway? Soon's I get my dough, I'm outta here.'

We didn't say anything for a while. She turned and kissed me. I kissed back. One thing led to another. She was different this time, more personal. After, we lay on the blanket, taking in the tune of the lapping water. The dark subsided and the tip of the sun came over the horizon. The vodka was left idle on the ground but the temptation had eased. She lay against my stomach and a car passed on the road behind us, its engine breaking the serenity. I took her hair and let it fall through my fingers. It was soft and it melted on my palm and then spilled away like a tender echo of whispering silk. Dawn came, forcing us to leave the night behind.

Chapter Three

Weeks passed and I saw her a lot more. As a recovering alco, you're warned not to let your grade accumulate. The thinking is that you might crack and have enough reserve to drink yourself into a coma. I spent my dough on the town with her. The real gentleman. A drink for my girl and a tip for the barman. She could drink better than any guy I ever knew, but I didn't care. I'd spend four hundred on a night out and rob it again by the weekend. She had class, a real beaut, and every guy in the damn place knew it. If there were other lovers, I didn't want to know. And she didn't say. It was a tacit agreement. And for a while. It was perfect.

And then it all went to fuck.

I was hanging around that afternoon, a real city buzz in the air. Shoppers and tourists and school kids eating lunch. A smell like wine drenched wood. Checked out my phone. One new voice message. She wanted to meet at my house later. I never brought a woman home. Didn't like people knowing where I lived. Rang back and spun some shit about wet paint. We agreed on Eyre Square. Went to Forster Court for a shower. A couple of kids hung around the alley drinking. One tried to sell me a television.

Met her that evening outside Richardson's. Looking casual. Low top. Loose dress and hair in braids. Eyes caught me again. Lemon aroma. Walked down Shop Street. Students falling around the place. Light rain. Went to a wine bar called BK's.

Interior. This was her type of place. Kat playing French tunes on a piano and a few crusty types in the corner. Said: 'Think I preferred Silverstrand.'

'It's ok. We're not staying.'

'What're we doin?'

The guy came to take the order. She was fluent in French. Figure that. He went to get it and she turned to me. 'I got something to tell ya.'

'Let's hear it.'

'Not here. Come for a walk.'

'Where?'

'The prom.'

He came back with two bottles of wine in brown paper bags.

Exit Bk's.

Exterior. Prom. It was a cloudless night and the tide was out. There was a light warm summer breeze. We sat on the ground beside the diving board. She opened a bottle, drank from the neck and said: 'We're finished, Charlie. What the fuck are we gonna do now?'

'I don't get ya.'

'I'm getting my grade in about two weeks.'

'All of it?'

'All €50,000.'

She took some wine. Its aroma gave me an image of dew falling over dawn Vineyards in France. Sat back with my palms on the sandy ground and squinted at a light in the distance. She pushed her hair back from her eyes and asked: 'What're ya thinking?'

'That this is the end of the line.'

'For us?'

'Yeah.'

'I never lied to you.'

'I know.'

'And we had some good times.'

'Short and sweet.'

'A happy ending depends on where you stop filming.'

I crossed my legs, yoga style, palms still on the ground.

She asked: 'So, what're you gonna do?'

'Steal and read.'

'That's it?'

'That's it.'

'There's more to life, Charlie.'

'Not for me.'

'Yeah there is.'

'I doubt it.'

'You have to see the world.'

'I've seen enough to last me.'

'Ballinrobe and Galway?'

'People are people, no matter where you go.'

'I think you're afraid.'

'Bollocks.'

'Then come with me.'

'Where?'

'Travelling.'

'That ain't my scene.'

'You don't know that.'

'I'm a home bird, babe.'

'You're afraid.'

'Fuck you.'

Pause. 'Yeah, you do that Charlie. Get aggressive and shove it back down to where you don't have to think about it.'

'Maybe you're just runnin from life.'

'Maybe. But if I am I won't deny it, and I'll have a helluva good time along the way. I'll die laughing. You'll either fall off the wagon or end up in jail for stealing handbags.'

Instrumental.

I broke it. 'We're loners, babe, on the margins. We don't do this shit. We just walk away into solitude.'

'We can do what we want. Don't let the world fuck you over just because you were dealt a bad hand.'

'I'll think about it.'

'That means no.'

'It means *I'll think about it.*'

'You go think, Charlie. And you keep thinking, and thinking more, and then when it's too late, you'll blink and I'll be gone. And then you'll curse the day you ever fucking thought at all.'

I stood up, lit a smoke and said: 'I'll call you tomorrow.'

Slept bad that night. Had grotesque nightmares. Felt like I was back in the horrors. The bed was cold, hadn't slept alone in a while. Woke up with a crazy desire to devastate my body with vodka, but knew she was right. There was nothing left for me in Galway. I had nothing to lose. I called her round lunchtime. She answered real casual with: 'Niño.'

'It's Charlie.'

'Sleep well?'

'No. You?'

'With the help of the wine.'

'I want outta here. You still want company?'

'I wouldn't have asked otherwise.'

'There's one thing, I wanna bring some of my own dough.'

'Don't worry, partner. I got us covered.'

'Still, I wanna pay my own way. I'm old school, and if it fucks up between us out there, I'll need a Plan B.'

'That's sweet, Charlie, real sweet. Well you got three weeks to rob all the wallets you can.'

'Why three weeks?'

'Cos there's a full-moon party in Thailand.'

'What the fuck is that?'

She sighed and hung up.

I looked at the phone and shrugged.

Dialled P.J. He answered with: 'Well...well...well?'

'Fuck the small talk. What's the story with that job?'

'Straight to the point, I like your style. We're still on track, Friday night, you want in?'

'I'll call you later.'

Click.

Exterior. Headford Road Retail Park. Late afternoon. Woodies gave the temperature at Eighteen degrees. Odds on for a good summer. Wanted to get the run of Chartbusters. Just in case something fucked up. These guys could be under cover for months and then Charlie gets thrown into the bargain too. Fuck that. The mention of Kramer's name triggered a lotta memories. I hadn't seen him in years but I'd heard the stats. He was doing well now, in the criminal sense. Had the largest operation in the city. Took out all the big players. General style. Crucifixions.

That kinda thing. We came up together from Ballinrobe in the old days, plying the same trade. But he'd moved on. And now he was king of the castle.

Inside Chartbusters. It was busy. There were shelves of Videos, DVDs and Playstation games. Went to the desk. Kat behind it, tag on his shirt, said — Supervisor: **Dave**. Wanted to suss around, needed to send him somewhere, said: 'Lookin for *On the Waterfront.*'

'Good flick, DVD?'

Knew it would take longer to find the tape, said: 'Ain't upgraded yet, still on the old VHS.'

Thought I detected a sigh. 'I'll take a look out back.'

Exit Dave. Tapped the wood real casual. Scanned the place. Lot of space. Camera in every corner. Checked out the opening times. Closed at midnight. Figured: get in around two, out by ten past. Fuckin P.J better have the plan worked out. Counted five cash registers, all looking handsome. Long day, lots of fucks coming in, no jobs, smoking dope, buying flicks. Dave came back and said: 'Gotcha.'

'What's the damage?'

'€2.50.'

'Not bad for Brando.'

'Be more for the DVD.'

Slipped him a twenty. He was fast with the buttons but I clocked a lot of grade inside. 'And €17.50 change.'

'Thankin you.'

'Try have it back by Friday if you can.'

Gave him a wink, said: 'No problem.'

Faced for the door. Took a notion and hit upstairs. Watched through the steps for curious eyes. Negative. It was a tanning salon. The walls on the right were like a post-modern circus. All colours and arty. Pictures of tanned punters with big smiles, sitting on beaches. Got to the top. Smelled like something cosmetic with a taste of varnish. Wooden floors. Dark lighting. My steps echoed. Door at the end, coded. No good. Came around on the left flank. The sunbeds were like incubators. Long, sleek and somehow sinister.

Woman behind the counter. Stereotype. Filing her nails. I asked: 'What time do ya close?'

She didn't look up, said: 'Five minutes.'

Looked behind me. Saw a sign for the W.C. Asked if I could use the facilities and she pointed like a mute. I shrugged and walked over.

Interior. Two bathroom doors and an exit sign pointing to the right. Walked through. Came to a stairs. Dirty air came up to meet me. Glass door at the bottom with a bar at the front. Pushed it open. It led to a cold narrow side alley for deliveries. Smelled like diesel and gravel and exhaust fumes and wet cardboard and urine. And it was out of sight from the main entrance. Thought: that's all I need to know. Saluted the secretarial bitch on the way out. She didn't even look up. Made a mental note to piss on her desk the next time I was around.

Exterior. Early evening. Light breeze. Emotion: lucid and cold, like an assassin. Bought gloves in Woodies and a steel bat in Staunton Sports. Called P.J and told him I was in. He invited me over to discuss the plans.

Interior. Whitestrand Park. P.J's flat. He greeted me with a handshake and led me up the stairs. He was wearing a baseball cap and blue jeans and two earrings on his left ear. The place smelled like sweat and dirty laundry. Took a seat on the couch. Box in the corner, rabbit ears on top and shit reception. Sparked a smoke and threw him the pack. He caught it and said: 'What changed your mind?'

'Like you said, it makes life interestin.'

He shrugged and continued with: 'Joe's on the way.'

'You sure he's solid?'

'Yeah, like a rock. Made his bones years ago.'

'You work with him before?'

'Loadsa jobs. He's got a big mouth and likes to throw his weight around, but when the pressure's on, you can count on him. You wanna beer?'

'No.'

'Didn't think so.'

Exit P.J. Heard him rattle around the kitchen. Fridge open. Fridge closing. The hiss of a can being opened. Checked out the posters on the wall, *Goodfellas* and Bob Marley. He returned, slugging deep, said: 'You know, if this works out, we could make it a regular thing.'

I dragged, said: 'No way, man. Just a once off boost in cash for the summer.'

'I don't know, Charlie. Sometimes it's hard to turn them down.'

'That's the secret to stayin this side of the bars.'

'Think about it. It's all ours. Kramer doesn't take a cut of the heists as long we sell enough snow in the month. It's tax free in every sense of the word.'

'He know I'm on the job?'

'No. You wanna stay incognito?'

'Yeah.'

He drank, rasped and said: 'It's ok with me.'

Audio. P.J's phone. It was Joe. He was outside and wanted entry. He came up, looking ridiculous. Dressed in a tracksuit and a leather jacket. Gave me a shake, light and meaningless, then took one of my smokes without asking. I let it slide.

P.J threw him a can and we got down to the plans. Consisted of a map across the kitchen table. We pored over it. It was awkward, sketched in biro but it had the essentials. P.J played the General, pointing us through the plan of attack, whiff of beer on his breath. Afterwards, Joe stood up, wiry, said: 'Fuckin child's play.'

'That don't mean we can act like we're in playschool.'

'I agree,' said P.J. 'I want everyone clean on the night. No coke, no booze. Clear heads.'

'Don't look at me, man. I been clean for years.'

We both looked at Joe. He said: 'I'm not fuckin stupid, P.J.'

I said: 'Just don't prove yourself wrong.'

'I'll kick *you* fuckin stupid.'

I squared up. 'I'll put that down to inexperience. But after the job, if you still want a shot, you're welcome to it. But I'll tear ya to fuckin pieces.'

'Hey, hey, hey,' said P.J. 'Fuckin relax, we're all in it together. Charlie, calm the fuck down. Joe; shut the fuck up.'

Joe tried to stare me out and failed, said: 'I'm goin outside for a smoke. It stinks of bullshit in here.'

He left and I looked back at the plans. 'So that's it. Out the way we came in. Six minutes flat.'

'Yeah. We got a key for the front door and at least a nine minute window before the cops arrive. That's their average response time to an alarm call cos mosta them are hoaxes anyway. Sorted out by the time they get there. Child's play ain't a bad description.'

'Little prick. What about the lock on the shutter?'

'We need to break it. Shouldn't be a problem.'

'And you're sure the dough's gonna be there?'

'Every Saturday mornin, Brinks Allied come to collect. Cash doesn't leave the shop until they arrive.'

'So we're gonna visit first?'

'That's the idea.'

'You got a code for the safe?'

'It ain't got a code. It's a key lock.'

'Gonna blow it open?'

'No.' He pointed at the map, said: 'Key's locked in this office here. We break in, get the key, open the safe and disco.'

'What about wheels?'

'Sort that on Friday evenin.'

'Looks like we got it all wrapped up.'

'Yeah. But you don't so sound sure?'

'I'm paranoid about things that look too easy.'

'Sometimes you get a good hand, all you gotta do is make sure you don't fuck it up.'

'That's what worries me about Joe.'

'Take my word, he'll come through.'

'I fuckin hope so. You got a plan B?'

'We don't need one.'

Took from the tone that he'd had enough questions. Decided to split. Made some final arrangements and left. Met Joe on the stairs. We said nothing, just kept going. I walked into the night, wondering how the fuck I'd ended up back in a world that had nearly killed me.

Chapter Four

I waited for them in my room. Took in some Pink Floyd, *Hey You*. Great tune. Lay on the cot and smoked a Marlboro. The chemicals floated to the ceiling and I made shapes in the stains around the light. It was one 1.45. They were due at 2. I felt ready. Thought about El Niño. Didn't tell her bout the job. Didn't see the need. And besides, she'd've wanted to come along or something.

Finished the cig. Checked for everything. Had gloves and steel bat. The night outside was quiet, open like the mouth of the unknown. Locked my door and went downstairs to wait. Thought: these fucks better be on time. Heard the motor outside. Checked. Affirmative.

P.J driving. Joe beside him. Wheels were solid. Honda Integra, two-litre fuel injected. Excellent take-off. Custom designed for the purpose at hand. We said nothing, just drove. Joe smoked John Player Black and the air was thick with bad nicotine. Chemical Brothers playing *Believe*. Took a right at Al Muretto and came down by Prospect Hill. Wet streets, empty night. Sang into the car park and pulled up to put on the gear. P.J threw me a balaclava, said: 'Like we agreed, no fuckin around. In, find the shit and out.'

Joe said: 'Sir, yes sir.'

P.J hit him on the shoulder. 'I'm fuckin serious.'

We put on the masks. Got out. Smell of petrol. Had my bag to carry the grade. Joe had the key, cut by the contact. He was looking agile, wild. Suspected he was coked up.

Faced with the shutter. Padlock at the bottom. P.J had a hammer, gave it two swings on the head. It broke easy and came up with a screech. Image: silhouettes reflecting from the glass. Entered. Switch to night shot. Placed smelled sterile and dusty. Joe's job was to keep watch. Me and P.J were to get the cash. There were cardboard film stars everywhere, staring down, looking real. Heart was going, fire in the belly; back in action.

We jumped the counter and searched for the room upstairs. Found it. Heard a crash, thought: fuck, the pigs ain't that fast. Checked it out. It was Joe. Breaking shit, tryna act real psycho. Pulling stuff off the shelves, stamping on it. Made a mental note to break his head later. Destruction wasn't in the game plan, could bring unwanted attention. Clocked an alarm in the corner. Silent, flashing red; fuzz were already on the way. Turned to P.J. said: 'This is what you call comin through?'

'Let's get the shit and talk about it later.'

He shouted at Joe to shut the fuck up and we took the stairs in threes. Found a door at the top that said: Personnel Only. Gave it the best with my weapon. Didn't give. Took three more times and a couple of kicks from P.J. Inside was a typical office. Computers, photocopier, fans. Smell like fresh paint. A desk with locked drawers. Cracked the top one open and the key glittered inside.

Sweating, legs going. Breath meets balaclava. Adrenaline overdrive. Found the safe in the next room. It opened on the first twist and the grade fell out. Looked sweet. Heard voices downstairs. Shouting, arguing. Fuzz were in. P.J ran down. Heard a scuffle, threats, more sirens.

I lodged the cash in bundles.

P.J. came back. Panting, frantic. 'Joe just nailed a cop. There's about twenty more outside. We're fucked.'

Closed the bag, said: 'Shut the fuck up and follow me.'

'Where?'

'Plan B.'

Enter landing. Door to the left. Kicked it open. Saw the sunbeds and ran through. Down the stairs, hung at the exit door and watched the activity outside. Squads pulling up. All lights and panic, running inside after Joe. Real fuckin heroes, walkie-talkies squawking. Saw the last one go in and bolted for the Integra. Night air against the face. Bag heavy on the shoulder. Commotion to the right. Got to the wheels and left them for dust. We were over the bridge by the time they knew what the fuck had happened. Joe was in shit street, but that was his problem. We burned the car at the docks and went back to the pad.

Interior. P.J's flat. Early hours. Smelled like dried grease. Spilled the loot on to the kitchen table. Lit smokes and did the count. The feel of hard cash, crisp notes between the fingers. The beautiful sight of high denominations. When we finished, it was bright outside, the money stacked in confident piles. Time to talk about the split. We had just over forty eight grand. I said: 'Way I see it, stack of sixteen each.'

'Not that easy.'

'Au contraire. It's precisely that easy.'

'The kid wants a cut for settin up the job.'

Thought: fuck him; I didn't see him wearing no mask, asked: 'How much?'

'Three.'

'Leaves it at fifteen. I'll take mine now.' I reached over.

P.J smoked, said: 'Joe hit that pig pretty bad. I don't think he's comin back.'

'Do what ya like. He's a prick and I don't like him. But a job's a job, and that's his cut. I'm takin mine and gettin out.'

'Still with the old code?'

'It ain't old to me. It's just the way it is.'

'Kramer never forgot it either.' Said nothing, he continued. 'He still respects what you did that time.'

'I'd expect the same from him. You think Joe'll talk?'

'No. He'll do time, but he won't say nothin. It's all part of the business.'

'You said we could trust him too.'

'Any doubt and he'll be wiped out before he can do any damage.'

'I think the damage has been done.'

He ignored it, said: 'You should give Kramer a call; he's got a lotta of work.'

'I'm busy enough, but I'll keep it in mind.'

'I'll send him your regards.'

'Incognito, remember?'

Took my stack and we said our goodbyes. Walked a quiet route back. Cops probably still on the prowl and I was taking no chances. The money was heavy inside my coat but it felt good, like meeting an old friend.

CHAPTER FIVE

Your time is the only thing you truly own, why sell it to someone else? This is what I thought about saying to Detective Inspector John Malone when he arrived at my door. He wanted to know if I'd been working lately. The guy was a real cliché. He had the slacks, the brown shoes, the tweed, and a tie like a fuckin kaleidoscope. He even had a moustache and the beady eyes to go with it. Under normal circumstances, I'd've figured someone was taking the piss.

Instrumental. I broke it with: 'That's all you wanted to know?'

'Among other things.'

'Kind of in a hurry, chief.'

'Tea be nice.'

Pretended to think about it. Looked at my watch, shrugged and let him in. Boiled the kettle. Fantasising about ways to torture Joe, asked: 'Sugar?'

Expected him to say something like: *no thanks, I'm sweet enough.* Instead, he said: 'Two spoons and a small dash of milk.'

Stirred the leaves and led him to the living room. He was looking around all suspicious. Chartbusters case on the table. Thought: fuck.

'What's the film?'

'*On the Waterfront.*'

'Good choice.'

Things were taking a shitty twist. Stayed deadpan. Tried to stare him out. 'You watch many movies, Charlie?'

Blew the steam off the top of my mug, sipped and said: 'When I get the chance, ya know. Busy man lately, college and all.'

He replied real pensive. 'Ah, college.'

Slurped his tea, left it on the ground. Brushed off his slacks and lit a smoke. Didn't ask or offer. Took out my own and sparked. We expired in silence, like someone was gonna draw. The he asked: 'You been staying quiet?'

'As always.'

'Had any visits lately, from your J.L.O?'

Juvenile liaison officers - the kats that watch your moves after you fuck up.

'Been a few years. I ain't so juvenile any more.'

He nodded, said: 'I see.' Crossed his legs. 'I read your file, it's very interesting.'

'I'm sure it is.'

'You've been lucky.'

We stared through a cloud of chemicals. I said: 'This is the point where you lay your cards on the table.'

He blinked and looked out the window, then got all serious. 'I'm here to give you a choice, Charlie — something that can put you in the clear once and for all.'

He crossed his legs again and brushed some ash from his knee. I said: 'That's great, chief, and I appreciate it. But I've been in the clear for a long time now, so thanks for the favour, but I'll decline.'

'You haven't heard what I have to offer.'

'I don't care.'

'I think you might.'

I looked at my watch again. He took the hint. 'Plead guilty for the job on Chartbusters. Give up Kramer, P.J and the rest of the crew and I'll guarantee you a place on the Witness Protection Programme.'

Thought: this guy's a fuckin madman, said: 'You're a fuckin madman.'

'If you choose not to do it, then you'll go down with the rest of them, and I promise you Charlie, they *will* go down.'

'I ain't goin up, down, or sideways, coz I ain't done nothin. I'm clean as a fuckin whistle. You know it an I know it.'

'Joe has a different story.'

'Who's Joe?'

'Are we going to play this charade all morning?'

'If you got the time, chief. Fact is, you'll find nothin. We can play it all fuckin day.'

He pointed, said: 'You purchased that film on Wednesday. The place was hit Friday night. We have your build on CCTV the night of the robbery. We know your connection to Kramer and lets not forget Joe. The walls are closing, Charlie. It's time to bail out.'

'Is this the point where I say: cuff me, John, it's all my fault?'

He sat back and shook his head. More silence, then: 'You read the papers lately? We had Joe cracked before he even made it to the station. There's a warrant out for P.J's arrest right now and next stop Kramer. There's an officer in a coma, son, and heads are going to roll.'

'Well rehearsed, detective.'

'Your friends have become both greedy and stupid, but you can save yourself.'

'They're not my friends.'

'We know you're not a big player, but we can make it look otherwise for a judge.'

He let the threat sink in. I said: 'Was that all?'

'I'm giving you a week to think about your options.'

'You can hear my answer right now if ya like.' He stared, blinked, I said: 'Go downtown. Buy some new threads. Get a hair-cut and go fuck yourself.'

He walked to the door, pulled it open, looked back and said: 'I'll see you in seven days.'

Interior. Mind. Rapid thoughts. Needed a place to stash the dough, possible warrant on the way. Could say a good day at the tracks but they wouldn't buy it, fits too easy into the stolen bundle. Fuckin Joe. Thought about calling P.J but didn't want to stir the shit. Could be all a hoax from Malone, playing us off against each other til someone cracks. Phones tapped and spill everything right into their big hairy ears.

Left for a paper.

Interior. Centra shop on Forster Street. Tabloids screaming from the ground, real witty bastards with a headline like — *Coked up Junkie Joe sends Cop into Coma.* Did a quick scan through. Details of the damage and talk about two kats that escaped. Quote from Dave saying: *"We're all shocked...this is terrible..."* that kinda shit. Talk about the patient — serious condition but stable.

The heat was on. Malone even had a line: *"No expense, time, or manpower will be spared in tackling these social fungi. Justice will be done."*

Social fungi? Fuckin knob.

Exit shop. Time to make a call. The day was cool with a dark edge. Lost-looking kats walking round with grocery bags. Tourists asking stupid questions and taking pictures. A kid came up, tall but looked young. Tracksuit and stupid hairstyle. Saw the question coming. 'Will ya get us twenty Benson inside?'

'What age are ya, son?'

'Sixteen. But the law's gone up two years.'

'Sorry, kid, I ain't the government.'

'Ah, go on.'

Shook my head, said: 'Can't do it. Against my principles.'

'Fuck your principles. It's only twenty fags.'

Thought about it, something inside said no.

'No.'

He winced and said. 'Bollocks.'

Took out my smokes and his face lit up. Sparked myself and asked: 'Want one of mine?'

'Yeah.'

He reached over. I pulled back and blew a cloud in his face, said: 'Now I'm a bollocks.'

Left him looking wounded. Turned and dialled.

Phone voice – soft.

Image: luscious lips against the mouthpiece. Always imagined her dressed in black. 'Alright, babe?'

'Well Charlie, how'd you do?'

'Don't get ya.'

'We got results this morning.'

'Results?'

'Yeah. We got degrees now.'

'Heard nothin.'

'Came in the post.'

'Never checked. Had a visitor.'
'Ask me how I did.'
'How'd you do?'
'Ok.'
'Only ok?'
'No. I got a first.'
'Fuck off.'
'It's a fact.'
'Congratulations.'
'Go check yours and call me back.'
'Will do. But I need a favour.'
'Hit me.'
'Don't like talkin on the waves.'
'I'm intrigued.'
'Meet me at the college in an hour. By the library.'
'I'll be there. Go get your results.'
Click.

Meanwhile back at the ranch. Had the cash in a shoebox under the bed. Put it in a bag and played a student. Checked for my grades on the way out. Found a tall rectangular letter. Cut it open. Two sheets. One to say congrats, the other with the scores. Scanned to the bottom — second class honours, grade one. Clicked my tongue, said: 'That'll do.'

Took the scenic route to the college. Thing about heat being, it raises your senses, so you're in tune, like prey looking out for a predator. Your antenna's always twitching for danger. Went by Tonery's car park and down Prospect Hill. Straight on through the Dyke road and over the Bridge. Any kats following would have to be on foot.

She was already there. Hair tied back and eyes wide. Black leather jacket and blue jeans. She opened with: 'I hear there's snow on the roofs in Petrograd.'

'Don't worry. We got plenty of heat to melt it.'
'So what's the deal?'
'Bag of cash. Need a safe house.'
'How much?'
'Over fifteen large.'

'Sweet. Musta been a big wallet.'

'You don't wanna know. You got a good spot?'

'We could bury it in the garden?'

'What about an attic?'

'Yeah.'

'That'll do. Don't want to be lookin for shovels in a hurry.'

Spotted the shoes on the power lines again. Said: 'Let's get goin.'

Interior. Laurel Park. Wrapped the grade in plastic and she showed me the attic. Dust and steel cables. An old box of junk and a clock and a dead rat. We tip-toed across the rafters. Careful not to fall through. There was a smell like rotten furniture. She said: 'You sure the plastic is sealed tight?'

'Yeah.'

'You've done this before?'

'Welcome to the underworld.'

'It's kind of exciting.'

'When ya get away with it. Jail ain't that pretty.'

'I thought you never went down.'

'Heard the stories....' I spotted the water system, said: 'Behind there.'

It fitted nice. Like it was custom designed. We went back down the ladder and pulled the trapdoor shut.

Interior. Kitchen. The fresh air was a relief. She asked: 'So what's my crime?'

'Handlin stolen money. Accessory. That kinda thing.'

'And what now?'

'Need time to think. And make a plan.'

'Who's chasing? The cops or the robbers?'

'The fuzz.'

'They have anything solid?'

'They mighta got a guy with a loose tongue. But they could be bluffin too.'

'What if they're not?'

'That's what I gotta think about.'

Pause. Then she asked: 'How the results go?'

'Second Class, Grade One.

'Smooth. Let's celebrate.'

'How?'

'I got wine and ice cream.'

'Wine ain't much good to me.'

'I'll drink for the both of us.'

'Here?'

'I'll put a fire down inside. Pull the curtains and play it by ear.'

Interior. Sitting room. Cosy fire. Dark outside. She said: 'So you wanna tell me about the shit you're in?'

'Maybe later, when things unfold. You been lookin at maps?'

'Yeah, charting our course all day.'

'Great. Whatever. Galway's over for me.'

'Passed the crescendo myself. Anyone gonna miss you?'

'No-one important. But there could be a few loose ends.'

'Like this thing with the money?'

'Yeah, I gotta think of a worst case scenario. It involves more dangerous people than the fuzz.'

'Define dangerous.'

'Nothin I can't handle.'

'Then why mention it?'

'Coz somethin stupid could happen.'

'Lay low till we go.'

'I intend to.'

'Stay here and hide out.'

'Temptin. But I don't want people usin you to get to me.'

'Jesus, what're you into?'

'Nothin heavy just yet.'

She took up her smokes. Lit one using a match. The flame illuminated her face. A smell of sulphur lingered. She dragged hard. Exhaled. 'They won't beat you, Charlie. No matter who they are.'

'Thanks for the faith.'

'You're too smart.'

'You're the one with the first.'

'Your survival instinct is too strong. They'll reap a whirlwind.'

We spent the rest of the evening naked and entangled, surfing a long spectrum of pace and sensuality. Woke up in the morning and lit a smoke from the ambers of the dying fire. It tasted good, like a decision. I thought about the future. It was all happening together. Now was the time to make a move. Malone was right, the walls were closing and it was time to bail out, just not his style. My phone rang with the call I'd been waiting for but never wanted. It was P.J.

Kramer wanted a meeting.

But now a new history commences: a story of the gradual renewing of a man, of his slow progressive regeneration, and change from one world to another – an introduction to the hitherto unknown realities of life.

Fyodor Dostoyevsky, *Crime and Punishment*

CHAPTER SIX

Exterior. Cummin's car park, Ballinrobe. December. It's Saturday night and the town is busy. Late hours. Niteclub just over. Smell of fast food and drunk potential. I'm walking down Church Lane and there's a guy with a girl against the wall. She's left her bag on the ground and I'm thinking credit cards and cash. Could be my best score of the night. She's blonde, shoulder-length hair, seductive and slender. Her legs are wrapped around him, and she's moaning, like she's in a pleasurable dream.

My stomach flips as I walk too close to be social. Enter excitement and danger. I'm in the zone, like overtaking a car on a corner. The guy is a big farmer type. Check shirt and broad shoulders. Could do without a fight. I stop, like I'm tying my shoelace, stand up, take the bag and walk. Instinctively, I know they've both opened their eyes. I'm close enough to hear her ask: 'You got anything?'

'Yeah. Here?'

'No, somewhere quiet.' She stands up and slurs. 'Where's my bag?'

They look around and she says: 'Oh my god, where is it?'

He sounds like a real red neck. 'Fuck the bag. It's probably still inside.'

I look back and she senses me looking and I turn away. But it all comes together anyway. The red neck shouts: 'Hey! Hey you, c'mere!'

I keep my head down. Decide not to run until I'm outta sight. And that's when the cops come around the corner. The guy is running up to me now. Shouting, pointing, ready to kill. She's trying to keep up, but she can't coz she's wearing heels. There's this rhythm of *clip, clop* and *scrape* on the path. The police are looking like they know something's wrong. I take off against a rush of wind and adrenalin.

Round the corner, there's a man urinating against the wall and a couple arguing across the road. They all stop and observe the pursuit. But they're too slow to stand in my way. The siren comes on and the patrol car flies outta the lane behind me. My feet are thumping off the ground like heartbeats as I get to The Bowers gate and bomb it down the hill. It's dark and I can't see a damn thing, but I just keep going. The squad screeches to a halt opposite the entrance, then takes off again. I figure they're gonna try and close me down at the exit.

And this guy's still running after me. And he's fast and I'm thinking he's a football player or something. The descent is steep, like I'm running into the underworld. I keep as straight as I can and hope for the best. Only some dim light coming from the full moon above.

I reach the bottom and get tripped up. Hit the ground hard, knees and palms grazing on the gravel. Even saw stars. I spin on to my back. The handbag flies and I'm waiting for the handcuffs. Elbows are sore but I'm warm with racing blood. Figuring I'm pumped with a jaw breaking right hand. Just a matter of who comes first.

Somewhere, people are laughing. I'm panting hard and stand up to see the farmer come flying down. He falls too, worse than me, screaming as he rolls over. All I can see now are dark faces, holding flagons of cider and smoking cigarettes. They're shouting abuse and one of them gives him a kick. He groans on the ground. They pound him some more. On the head. On the stomach. On the legs. He covers his face with his hands til they stop. Then he struggles to get up. Not knowing what the hell is going on. He looks at me with a bloody nose. Then at the handbag. He's breathing heavy and I can tell he's scared. One of them shouts: 'Get the fuck outta here!' and kicks him again. He falls backwards then catches his balance and scrambles up the scared hill.

Silence. One of the gang steps forward and asks: 'You ok, man?'

I tell him I'm ok. He sparks a smoke and the flame brings out his features. He's got the face of someone you think you've known your whole life. It goes dark again and my eyes take a second to re-adjust. There's a vague scent of sulphur in the air. He says: 'I've seen you around. You're in the trade.'

I tell him I don't what he's talking about and he says: 'Yeah, ya fuckin do.'

I go to leave and he asks: 'You want a beer?' I say no and he says: 'Have a fuckin beer.'

He throws me a can. I catch it with both hands. It feels chilled. The moon comes out from behind the clouds and I can see them better. Leather jackets. Silver chains hung on blue jeans. He introduces them all. They're older, stronger, and in a bigger league than me. Much bigger than wallets and bags. He has a tough edge. Tattoos and arms like a bear. Tight hair with pierced ears. If I were to describe him in a word, I'd have to say charisma. He tells me his name is Kramer.

I open the can and swig. It's icy on the tongue and hits the chest hollow. I get settled and the banter is good but I don't say much. Three cans later and I'm thinking my welcome is over. I go to walk. He comes over again and asks if I'm looking for some real work. I say thanks, but no thanks. He says: 'You should think about it. Christmas comin, extra hands are always welcome.'

I tell him I'll think about it.

A couple of nights later I was back in The Bowers. Drinking hard and feeling like a real criminal. Up until then I was small time, but prided myself on my independence. No ties. No split. Maximum profit. Also, working alone meant you never had to pay for the mistakes of someone else.

The more I drank with the gang, the more I learned about Kramer. He was an orphan. Abandoned on a doorstep when he was a month old. After some failed foster homes, he'd spent his youth in an industrial school, learning how to survive in a world that had rejected him. The philosophy of the institution was to instil discipline and conformity. It didn't work. Instead, it acted as an alternative education.

He grew up with the delinquent kids that were too young to go to prison. He learned to fight and steal and developed contempt for all authority. When he finally escaped, they were glad to see him gone.

Once he was out, he hooked up with some of the contacts he'd made inside. Over the years he developed a flair for tactics and planning, and eventually formed his own gang. They were friends and associates from the school, and some aspiring criminals from the street.

These were the guys I'd burst into running down the hill.

The gang hit rural places. Shops, pubs and rich houses. Kramer was the mastermind of every job. He chose the crew, the place and the time. The money and spoils were always split evenly among everyone. The few times the cops chased, they were left lost on the country roads.

It was mid-January before I relented to go on a job. We were drinking and playing cards at Kramer's place when he brought it up. I'd watched them over Christmas, coming home with stacks of cash, blowing more in a night than I'd make in a week.

He opened with: 'How're the wallets?'

'Shite. Sick of it. How you been doin?'

He lit a smoke, threw down a card. 'Doin alright. Some of the guys are gettin greedy. They want bigger cuts and it's causin friction.'

I filled a cup of cider, asked: 'What're ya gonna do?'

'Keep it the way it is. If they don't like it, fuck them.'

'Think it'll come to a head?'

'So be it.'

'When's the next job?'

'Supposed to be tomorrow. Place I been scopin since Christmas.'

'Supposed to be?'

'All the gang are outta town. Shame too, coz it's only a two-man set up.'

He threw down another card and took a swig of Jack Daniels. I had some more cider, asked: 'What's the exposure time?'

'Two and half minutes tops. Rural gig, five miles from the nearest copshop.'

'How much?'

'Twenty grand upwards.'

'Sweet.'

We were silent for a while. The interest in the game was gone. Eventually he said: 'I gotta beat around the bush all fuckin night?'

Next morning. Outside the shop in a stolen car. He ran through the plan one last time. I felt alert, ready for anything. He threw me a balaclava and we set to work.

Interior. Shop. Chimes rang overhead. Stink of stale sweets and cats. Radio screaming death notices. Old guy stacking salt in the back. He looked up, fixed his glasses, said: 'One minute please.'

Kramer jumped the counter and hit the till. Wad of notes inside. Geriatric was up straight away: 'Hey, what the hell d'ya think you're up to ta? Come out outta that!'

Kramer said: 'Sorry, granddad.'

'Come out I tell ya!'

He hobbled over, shouting: 'Mary! Mary! Ring the guards!'

Kramer was cool as a cube. He ruffled around some more. Found a tin of notes. Sign on the front of it said: GAA. Lottery. He cleaned it, said: 'Hate them football fucks.'

I stuffed my bag with cigarettes, bottles of wine, scratch cards and poorboxes. The guy was roaring now. Mary came out, bout the same age, musta been the wife. She saw the scene and got all Shakespeare about it. Hands on her chest, gasped for breath, blessed and said: 'Oh Jesus, Mary and Joseph. Tommy, what's happenin? Who are they, Tommy?'

He grazed Kramer's head with the walking stick. 'Little pups!' Kramer pulled the stick off him and held it to his throat from behind. 'I don't want to hurt ya, Tommy. So just do what I fuckin say.'

He tried to break free but it was useless. He shouted at Mary to run. She just started screaming. I told her to shut the fuck up and get the money from the safe. She tried to play confused, then Kramer took out his blade and put it to Tommy's jugular.

I roared at her. 'He'll fuckin do it! He's gonna cut him! Get the fuckin money ya stupid bitch. Money cunt, money now! Get it!' I had a wheel brace in my hand. Raised it to her head roared: 'Now!!!'

She gave in. I followed her to the back room. The light glared through the morning windows. I was shouting all the while. Christ, she was terrified. There was a large rug on the floor. She pulled it back with shaking hands. A trapdoor underneath. Dust and loose coins and two big money bags inside. The unlodged grade from the Christmas take-ins. She threw it at me. 'Here! Take what ye want. Just leave us alone. Here! Let him go!'

I yanked her back out by the hair. Money in the other hand. Tried to ignore her screaming.

Kramer was still holding Tommy. I held up the bags, said: 'Got it.'

'You get the smokes too?'

'Yeah.'

'Booze and all that shit?'

'It's all there.'

'Then let's get the fuck outta here.'

I pushed Mary away and Kramer threw Tommy on the ground and we got going. The chimes rang again on the way out. And Tommy shouting: 'Bastards! Get the gun, Mary. The gun!' The death notices hadn't even finished. I was feeling calm, but invigorated.

Got back to Kramer's and did the count while smoking stolen Marlboro. We were up nearly eighteen grand in cash and twelve hundred in miscellaneous. Did the split. Worked out nice. Wrapped it in a band and relaxed. Kramer spoke first. 'See what I mean?'

'About the wallets?'

'Yeah.'

'Smaller fall though.'

'Smaller buzz.'

'That old guy was a real challenge.'

'You did good.'

'Cheers.'

'No, I mean it, man. The way you handled that bitch. Fuck. That's what I want. Small numbers, fast jobs and a straight split.'

'So what's next?'

'I got a couple of things lined up.'

'Need any help?'

'Not for now. But there'll be more. If you're up for it?'

Took a long belt of vodka, said: 'Yeah. Fuck it.'

Money dwindles when you're boozing every day and playing sticks at a ton a frame. There was no school or college. No job. And fuck all to do. Vodka became my hobby. Dash of orange juice and a double voddy. Great kick to start a session. We'd all started hanging out in a bar on the east side called The Cider Tiger. It was real small and personal. Fire on, good tunes and a healthy pool table. It was mostly just the crew and a few old geysers that drank in the place. The man that owned it was called Paul. He was one of those guys who hated to see people wasting themselves. He was a block layer by day, ran the bar at night. Had known my father somehow. Always trying to give me work. He'd come in every evening and see me at the bar drinking and he'd shake his head. But I thought: what're ya gonna do? Start wit a brickie, spend the week laying stones, or do a few hours robbing and make the same capital?

After a while, more work came through from Kramer. All the time he was edging closer toward two-man jobs. It was simpler and more profitable. He always told me a couple of days in advance, which was enough time to sober up and get my shit together. The crew didn't like it. They wanted to know what kind of money we were making and why they weren't involved. In the end, Kramer wished them luck and told them he was going his own way. They were pissed but saw the logic. Smaller numbers appealed to their desire for bigger cuts. And they figured they'd learned enough to survive anyway. It also meant Kramer and I became a two-man outfit.

The money rolled in. We worked to precision on everything and it always came off. As time went on, the cops got more focused. They were under pressure from the people who were sick of being victimised. Gradually, all the members of the old gang got sent down and we learned from every one of their mistakes. We never left prints, never showed our face or called each other by name. We always burned the car after each job and, if there was any element of doubt, we never followed through on a plan. We weren't flash with the money and never talked to anyone about what we were doing. If a stranger came to The Cider Tiger, we always assumed he was undercover and made him feel unwelcome.

Although we stole for cash, we started to gather other valuables too. There was stuff from the houses like DVD players, televisions, video recorders and jewellery. Keeping it all around was like a neon fuckin sign for the law. We also had other shit from the shops like cigarettes, bottles of wine, scratch cards and home accessories like torches, microwaves and stereos. For all this, we had a fence. He was the guy who knew a fella that would buy your goods at a discount. He was like a middleman who laundered stolen merchandise. You sold the stuff to him at a knockdown price and he had a buyer waiting. Nobody asked questions. The only problem was where to store it all in the meantime.

Then. We were driving down the Creagh Road and discussing a job in Partry village. I was polishing off a bottle of vodka when Kramer hit the brakes hard and said: 'What the fuck?'

I wiped the drink from my shirt, asked: 'What?'

He was pointing at a small hut in the middle of a field. 'Check that out.'

He was out before I had time to argue. We walked over. It was spacious inside. Solid interior, blackened wooden walls and a high roof. Some rusted tools thrown around, but it was otherwise abandoned. Smelled like creosote. He said: 'What do ya think?'

'How d'ya mean?'

'Safe house.'

'Safe house?'

'Yeah.'

'What about the punter that owns it?'

'Looks like there's no one been here for years.'

He had a point. It was isolated enough not to be found and a perfect place to meet the fence. We got back to the pub that night and quizzed Paul about who owned the land down there. It had belonged to a farmer that had died. The inheritance was locked up in a family dispute. One side wanted to sell it and the other wanted to farm it. The hut used to be a halfway house for the guy's gear. It meant he didn't have to drag all his shovels and shit around. Paul said it would probably be years before anything happened with it. We moved all the stuff out the next day and I brought a few bottles of the wine home. Like every other aspect of our job, we resolved not to talk about it to anyone.

That night I puked blood on the bathroom floor and slept in the bath.

CHAPTER SEVEN

We started running out of places to hit. We'd done shops, pubs, and rich-looking houses – even warehouses – but it was never enough. We were like the crews in the movies. Always wanting the ultimate heist. We had a safe house full of all the materials we could ever need. But we still pushed for more. All the time we were going for bigger jobs and higher rewards. When Kramer got the tip about the post-office, we knew it was exactly what we'd been looking for. He told me over a game of pool on a Monday afternoon. I'd been drinking since morning.

'Post-office. Friday. Pension day.'

'Big jump from the shops.'

'It's all relative. Serious upgrade in cash too.'

'What's the location?'

'Headford.'

'What's the fuzz like up there?'

'Same as everywhere — fat and stupid.'

'We got a driver?'

'No. Two-man job. In, out, and gone in ten minutes.'

'How much you thinkin?'

'Eighty to a hundred.'

Whistled, said: 'In early?'

He potted the black again. I paid him another fifty. He shoved it in his jeans back pocket and continued: 'Yeah, the timelocks open in the mornin so they can take out all they need. On somethin like pension day, they're gonna need a shit loada dough to pay all the geriatrics.'

I was on vodka&redbull. Gulped it down and gave the signal at the bar for another, said: 'We ain't done nothin this big before.'

'Exactly.'

The drink came. He looked at it and said: 'I'll need ya dry for this one. No fuckin around.'

'I hear ya.'

'Tell me now if you're in, and you'll be sober. If not, I'll find someone else.'

'I'm good for it.'

'Don't fuck with me, Charlie. I'm not goin down over a fuckin hangover.'

'Don't worry about it, chief. Gimme the run down.'

We took a seat in the corner. 'Routine's like this. Timelock opens at 8.45 and a kat gets the cash ready for the mornin pay-out. Then he locks the safe again until lunch-time.'

'So we follow him in?'

'Yeah. He'll be there by 8.20. Small fuck with a bald head. Shouldn't be a problem.'

'That's the whole staff?'

'One other woman comes in about 9. But we'll be out by then.'

'And the safe just opens itself?'

'No. That's the glitch. When it's time, an alarm goes to let ya know that the door can be opened, but we still need the keys. We get them off the bald guy. After that, we have forty seconds to open the safe or it re-sets the timer for another fifteen minutes — that's what we want to avoid.'

'We're aimin for a forty second window?'

'Yeah.'

'Jesus. Couldn't we just wait til he takes the dough out himself, and then hit?'

'Thought about it. Two problems. First, he might not take it all out. I want all that's in there. And second, it'll take too long and increase the exposure time. This way, we'll have more time to get out before the public start arrivin and we won't have to deal with the other bitch.'

'What if she's the only one who knows where the keys are?'

'Two people need to know, in case one gets sick or somethin. The only risk is that the guy tries to play the hero and doesn't come across.'

We broke it down and figured we had all the angles covered. After, I was hit with a feeling of progression, like I'd just been promoted.

Interior. Nice wheels. Hyundai Coupe. Black. Kramer picked me up at my house on Friday morning. I was sober but my body creaked like I'd been hit by a lorry.

We spent the journey smoking and listening to the Manics. Twenty minutes later, we were sitting outside. It was 8.15. Things were getting busy on the street — delivery trucks, bread vans that kinda shit.

I felt worse than a sewer smells. Kramer reached into the back. Got something and said: 'Check this out.'

It was a shotgun. Single barrel. Serious potency. I asked: 'The fuck'd you get that?'

'The Fence. When he's low on cash he trades. Not bad, eh?'

'Not fuckin bad at all. Hope we don't have to use it.'

'I doubt it. Just figured. Bigger job. Bigger weapons.'

'Fuckin right.'

'You got your bat?'

I pulled it out. 'Yeah.'

There was some dirt and rain on the windscreen. Kramer flicked the wipers. The glass came clear and we saw the man with the plan. He was almost bald with glasses and a double chin. White shirt and a stomach with too many big lunches. Everything about him said he worked behind a desk and did fuck all.

We were out in sync. Car doors open and greeted by the cool morning air. Bat gripped in my hand and blood going. Both of us in overalls and balaclavas. The whole fuckin world was amplified. We watched him shove the key in the latch and it screeched like feedback. Something triggered and he turned. Saw the world through his eyes. Early morning routine, had done it for twenty years, no problems — and then we were on him like panthers. We pulled him through and shut the door. He tried to shout but I had his mouth covered.

Interior. Post-office. Smelled like eucalyptus. Plant in the corner beside a water cooler. Small counter, glass protected. Door beside it, said: STAFF ONLY.

Checked out his wallet. Kramer scoped outside for onlookers then came back. I said: 'His name's Frank.'

I let him fall to the floor and put a foot to his windpipe. Kramer put the gun to his face, said: 'I don't want to kill ya, Frank. I don't even want to hurt you, but if you don't do what I ask, I'll fuckin crucify ya. D'ya hear me?' He looked up with wide eyes, making gurgling noises. His hands were gripped round my leg. 'Now, we're gonna empty the safe, and you're gonna help us. When we let you up you'll be quiet and you'll give us the keys. You understand what I'm sayin?'

I stood back and he wobbled like jelly on the ground. Then he got up and fell sideways. Face green, like he was seasick. He used the counter for support and tried to say something, but it just sounded like a wheeze. His hands started shaking and he bent over, breathing heavy. I took aim with the bat. Legs apart like I was gearing up for a home run, said: 'Whenever you're ready, Frank.'

Kramer raised the gun, like he was taking aim at a distant target. 'Frank....'

Frank wiped a thick layer of sweat from his forehead and made another attempt to stand up straight. I was sizing up his kneecap when his eyes went crisis wide. We both knew something had gone terribly wrong inside him, like all the lights on the dashboard were flashing at the same time. We exchanged concerned looks. Then his face went a shade of purple and he collapsed like an alcoholic in a brewery. I was still poised with the bat, asked: 'What now?'

'Wait for the other bitch. Let's pull this fat piece of shit out back.'

We pulled him through to an office. He was like a horse in a coma. Left him on the floor. Blood on his nose, short wheezy breaths. Small gig inside. Computer, swivel chair, pictures of the family. I checked the time. It was 8.34, asked: 'She due soon?'

Looked at his watch. 'Round 9. She probably figures this fuckhead is on top of things.'

'Looks like a heart attack.'

'We'll deal with it later.'

Something started ringing and we went to check it out. Feeling edgy. Sorta cranked. Kramer held the gun all the time.

With that and the masks, it felt like we were terrorists. Found the safe in a room behind the main counter. It was square and bland; looked like an oven. The noise was coming from a bell on top to tell us the door was ready to be opened. Without the keys, we had to wait the fifteen minutes.

Her name was Evelyn. She was thin, wiry and brittle. Dressed in a pants suit and a scarf. Hair almost grey. She was well over sixty. Smelled of false teeth and bad perfume. I took her in a chokehold and covered her mouth. Kramer demanded the keys but she just kept trying to break free. I thought she was gonna snap in half. In the end, we pulled her back to the office and let her see Frank. Then we put the gun to her head and she was finally persuaded. Her hands were shaking wild and I thought we were gonna have two fuckin casualties. After, we tied her up and gagged her with a scarf and the timing bell rang again.

The outer door took two keys, to be turned at the same time. We pulled it back. It was heavy and slow, like a small Swiss vault. Looked like a fridge inside. Three compartments for cash, coins and stamps.

I was sweating like a broken reservoir. The dough was piled in stacks of thousands. I crooked my arm around the whole lot and let it fall into the bag. 'Get it all.' Said Kramer. 'All of it. Every fuckin penny.'

I did.

We got ready to leave. Kramer went to see if Frank was alive and I looked out the window. There were folks waiting, like a crowd of zombies, looking confused and trying the door. Kramer came back, asked: 'How we fixed?'

'Not the best.'

Looking through, he said: 'Fuck it. We'll have to run through them.'

We checked that there was nothing left behind. All clear. Evelyn watched us with scared eyes. Kramer showed her the barrel of the gun one last time, said: 'Hasta Luego.'

And then we pulled the door and ran.

Through an amazed audience.

They were too shocked to be scared. There were gasps and shouts as we jumped into the wheels. Later, they would claim they thought their lives were in danger. Kramer steered us out and we disappeared, into the distant realms of their imagination.

Drove like crazy to Inishmacatreer. Had another car waiting. The money was heavy. But the weight added to the high. I knew we'd scored big and felt fuckin bulletproof. Burned the wheels and went home for the split. Our biggest score to date. But at a higher price than usual.

–

The news had broken by lunchtime. The radio said they had no suspects. But it was possibly connected to a recent spate of robberies in the area and they were following a definite line of enquiry. The fat guy Frank had been rushed to hospital and was in critical condition. The old chick Evelyn was treated for shock but was at home safe with her family.

Everything was getting surreal, like we were watching ourselves from above. I asked Kramer: 'What if he dies?'

'Not our fault.'

'The law won't see it that way.'

'He was miserable anyway.'

'There's gonna be a lot of heat if he croaks.'

'I checked him before we left. He looked fine.'

'Doesn't mean he'll make it.'

'He'll make it. It was only shock.'

I opened a bottle of vodka and offered him a can from my stash.

'No thanks, man. I got somethin better.' He took out a joint, roached and ready-made. 'Got this shit off the fence aswell. You want one?'

'Not into that shit, man.'

'It'll help ya come down. Ease the tension.'

'Make ya fuckin stupid too.'

'Only if ya use too much.'

Thought about it. 'No thanks, I'll stick with the booze.'

'Bet ya fuckin will.'

'Fuckin will what?'

'Drink that shit. Spend all your grade on the piss for a fuckin hangover.'

He sparked the joint and the scent came through my tubes. Reminded me of funerals and relaxation sticks. Kramer inhaled real deep. I said: 'Shit stinks.'

'Tastes damn good.'

He dragged some more. 'Don't worry, Charlie, the fat fuck's gonna make it. The papers'll scream for a while, then it'll be old news.'

Had a bad vibe, like we'd gone too far, said: 'Still might be best to lay low for a while. We mighta pushed it a bit.'

'Fuck them.'

'And what about the woman?'

'What about her? She'll describe two guys in masks, nothin else. We're covered. I know what you're sayin, but I don't rate this as a problem.'

He finished the joint and rolled another. I made a good dent in the bottle. Was starting to share his optimism, like things might blow over. I asked: 'Any big plans for your dough?'

He licked the skin, said: 'I got a few ideas in mind. Things I been thinkin about for a while.'

'Like what? Goin straight?'

Laughing: 'Fuck that. I want the cities, man.'

'The cities?'

'Yeah. I wanna break into somethin bigger, maybe Galway. Today was only a taste of what can be made up there. What d'ya think?'

'They're all wrapped up with the local gangs. Harder cunts than us.'

'We could take 'em.'

I shrugged and said: 'Must be strong weed.'

He took a long drag. 'Like I said, I been thinkin this for a while.'

'Why fix it if it ain't broken?'

'You just said you wanna lay low, that they'll be watchin us now. Sounds pretty fuckin broken to me.'

I swigged some vodka, said: 'But we can handle the shit around here. We got no experience in the big leagues.'

'All we need is balls.'

'Real Tony Montana.'

'Worked for him.'

'Until he got fuckin wasted.'

'We all gotta go, Charlie. Secret is, live a dream in between.'

Chapter Eight

Frank at the post-office had had a diabetic stroke. He was brought to hospital right after the raid. He did some time in intensive care but they figured he'd make it. There was a public outcry. People were saying all sorts of shit. Like we beat him and tried to kill him. Radio stations were barking about manhunts and vigilante-style punishments. Everyone knew it was us in the end. That shit always leaks out. The cops started sniffing around Kramer's house. Asking questions about his income. One time he told them to go fuck themselves. They slapped him around bad and threw him in a cell for the night. After that, we knew enough not to try anything for a while. And besides, there was enough cash to keep us going.

Soon enough, Frank got out. A week later, they'd organised a news-special on organised crime. And its effect on the victims. Victims like Frank. The cameras went to his house. I watched it in The Cider Tiger.

They had one of those old homely joints. The type with a grandfather clock in the back. And a picture of the Pope on the wall. A cabinet in the corner with wedding photos of false smiles and hope for a future that never happened.

Wife on the screen. Frank in the back. Head lolled to the left. Saliva leaking from the side of his mouth. She was all passionate about hunting down 'the thugs'. Frank in the background, trying to hobble around with a Zimmer frame. Inching from the kitchen to the bedroom. They tried getting him to talk. But his lips were all warped and twisted, like he'd had a hard day at the dentist. Things were uncomfortable in the pub, like everyone was stuck watching a love scene with their parents. Frank had a daughter too. She was a real mouthpiece. Lots of cellulite and lipstick on her teeth. Said words like: *Actually*, and *literally*, all the time. I wanted it to be over. Gave a scan for the remote control.

The daughter had a man with her too. Looked like he sold houses and had a big car. Square head, trying to get his mug on the box. Good for business. He stayed dumb and tried to look thoughtful. She did all the yapping. As if she had it down about the social inequalities of the country. Like she wanted to say: "I know the score, I'm educated. This is what you should do."

One night in The Bowers. In the early days. A guy called Sweets. I don't why they called him that. Told me bout his first trip to the Industrial school. He was picked up at the courthouse. There was a priest driving. They didn't talk much. The car was new. He remembered that. Not long before they arrived, the collar got an idea. Pulled into a side road and raped Sweets in the mouth. Afterwards, he zipped up and kept going. Like it had never happened at all. I wondered if Frank's daughter knew anything about that.

The camera was real selective about what they showed. It was like our fifteen minutes. Cept we were never mentioned. It came back to the wife. They kept her head to the side of the screen so that Frank was always in the back. The daughter sat with him, in a pink suit. Spooning baby food down his throat. The sound track was Celtic and slow. When it ended, things were awkward in the pub.

I took offence.

Everyone shifted their feet and looked deep into their pints. I was well into a bottle of vodka by now. I picked up the cue, addressed them all: 'We playin fuckin pool or what?

A bored kid in the corner set them up. He was always here, cos his father was always here - drinking. That annoyed me. I slammed the glass on the counter. Flecks of ice flew like shrapnel. Place was cold, atmosphere dead. I rammed the white into the pack. It flew off the table, clipped the jukebox and walloped off the back door with a clunk. I looked at the worried kid, pointed the stick like a sword, said: 'Your fuckin shot.'

He picked up the white ball from the floor and proceeded with caution. I switched off the television and shouted for decibels on the jukebox. Put in a loada silver and logged about fifty tunes. Loud, hard, angry. Played an aggressive, careless game. Lost it, and the next one too. Didn't care. Bought drink for the house. Flogging a dead crowd.

Got through about two bottles of vodka. The kid beat me again. Sank a slick black into the top right hand pocket. I went up to his father, told him to bring his boy home. He was only about ten years old and this was no place for him. And men his age shouldn't be away from home for so long every day. Things happen. People break-in. Fires start. Wives get hurt. The man was scared. I could see it in his eyes and it felt good. He drained his pint and picked up his son and left without another word.

Sexy chick behind the bar, her name was Jane. She'd had enough and said: 'Charlie, I think you should leave.'

Smiled, used all the drunken sarcasm I could, said: 'That's great, Jane. And you're a real nice lookin girl and all, but ever try to say anythin like that again and I'll wrap this fuckin pool stick round your head. Now get me a fuckin vodka.'

She looked scared, filled a drink and disappeared out back. I racked up another game of pool. Was sorting out the balls in the triangle when Paul arrived, Jane behind him. 'That's your last drink, Charlie.'

'Fuck off, Paul. I'll finish when I'm finished.'

'That's your last, and you ever talk to my staff like that again and I'll break your fuckin neck. I don't care who your friends are.'

Customers turning their backs. Free drink buys no loyalty. Straightened up. Paul was in a real fuckin tantrum. Jane looked shit embarrassed. Cue in my hand, thought about giving it to him between the eyes. He read my mind. Pulled it away and threw me against a table. Glass smashed. Tables and chairs toppled over. He pulled me back against the counter. More stools fell, clattering off the ground. Jane screaming, all that. Tried to fight back, but my hands were knotted under his arms. Attempted a kick, then a head-butt. No use. He was a real swift mover. Had me outside in no time. Against the wall, slap on the face. 'The fuck are you doin, Charlie? Think you're a hard man? Causin shit in my bar, playin the real cowboy...the fuck do you think you're doin?'

'Better be careful Paul, or you won't have a bar anymore.'

'Don't even think about startin that shite with me. You think I don't see you drinkin yourself to shit? You think you can scare me like I'm some fuckin….diabetic?'

'Fuck you.'

Took me by the collar and shoved me back hard. Hit the wall, tough on the shoulder-blades. 'No, fuck you. I'm the one who's tryin to help ya. Give ya work and see ya right. And you pull this shit inside, throw it back in my face?'

'I don't need your fuckin sympathy.'

'Then get the fuck outta my pub. I don't wanna see ya round here again.'

He gave me a push up the street. I kept walking, all in a rage. Ready to kill, breathing heavy. Knew he'd take me out if I tried. Felt his eyes on the back of my head. He was breathing heavy too, said: 'Stay away from Kramer, Charlie. He's draggin ya down.'

Turned and gave him the finger, said: 'I don't know what the fuck you're talkin about.'

Exterior. Outside The Cider Tiger. I took a left, headed for home. Feeling hate for all the world. I had notions of robberies, kneecaps, arson. Somewhere close a siren wailed. Turned. Saw the big blue lights. Stripe along the side. Then it pulled up. Cop jumped out and walked with me.

'Well, Charlie?'

Real culchie with the belly and the chins. Yellow jacket. Looked like a fuckin road sign. 'Well what?'

'Where you off to this time of night?'

'Your place. Heard your wife's good.'

'I don't have a wife.'

'I'm not surprised.'

'Don't get lippy, Charlie. We'll make life awful hard for you.'

'Can't get much fuckin worse, chief. You want somethin or what?'

'Hands against the wall. Legs spread. Let's go.'

'Wha?'

'You heard me. C'mon.'

Some night, some fuckin show. He checked all my pockets. Patted me from head to toe. Found nothing. It was a rule me and Kramer had. And common sense too. Don't carry your whole fuckin stash around. The cop was disappointed, said: 'Take off your shoes.'

'My shoes? Is the pay that bad?'

Another one came from behind. Thinner. More a slice of gammon than the real thing. Walkie-talkie in the hand. He said: 'Not as good as the drugs trade, I'm sure.'

'Not my fuckin scene, Sarge. Like my drink, but that's where I draw the line.'

'We'll see. Shoes please.'

Late night Ballinrobe. Standing in your feet ain't a good idea. The breeze bites like a wasp, carries the bitterness of the whole damn town. You can almost hear the whispers of lost dreams and regret.

They went back to the car and got a fuckin dog. The mutt took a sniff. Found nothing. The first pig came back. Said something about me being lucky. But to watch myself. He went back into the car and number two came over. 'How's your friend Kramer now, Charlie?'

'Who?'

'Don't play stupid.'

'I didn't know this was a game.'

'We know he's started dealing.'

'Cards?'

'Drugs.'

'Drugs?'

'Yes.'

'And?'

'And we're just waiting for the right time.'

'To buy some?'

He threw me the shoes. 'To nail him. Go home, Charlie. We'll be in touch.'

Walked, rattled at events. My feet sore and cold. Thought about the drugs. That fence probably causing unwanted heat.

Still wanted more booze. Did a mental stock-take on my stash at home. Had vodka, wine, and stolen brandy. Should be enough. Craving set in, like a state of emergency. Got to the house. Went straight to the fridge and started on the cognac. Drank long and deep. The more it stung, the better I felt. Had some closing thoughts as the world went dark. It was time to get out. I'd call Kramer the next day. Fuck 'em all.

He was alone when I called. Shoved his head out. Did a quick scan and ushered me inside.

Interior. Kitchen. Empty bottles of Bucky and dirty pint glasses on the sink. Filthy plates and a smell of stale bread. Sounds coming from a small deck in the corner. Beats and piano, Mobyesque. Tile floor and cream walls. He took a seat by a nine-bar on the kitchen table. I whistled, said: 'Now I know why they wanted my shoes.'

'You too?'

'Yeah, last night.'

'Bastards were here as well.'

'They get anythin?'

'No. I got this shit today.' He pointed at it. 'Imagine fittin the size of that fuckin thing in your shoe?'

'They said you were dealin.'

'Small time.'

'Good dough?'

'Top dollars. Want to go halves? Be a distributor?'

'Told ya, man. I don't trust it.'

'You're missin out on some serious grade, Charlie boy. It's even worth the hassle from the pigs.'

I noticed he'd gained weight. 'Give it a name, I wanna get outta the Robe. I agree with what you said.'

'Bout Galway?'

'Yeah. I wanna move on. Try some work up there.'

He took a Stanley off the kitchen table. 'I been lookin into it, too.'

'And what's the story?'

'Got a contact. He can set us up with a gaff. Maybe introduce us to a few people.'

'Any idea when?'

'Need a week. After that, I'm good.'

Pointed at the smoke, asked: 'What about that shit?'

He carved a bit. Adept with the blade. 'I'm out of it after this. Good money yeah, but I want real work again — somethin that makes the heart beat faster.'

Told him to call and faced for the door. He held me with: 'Hey, Charlie, to keep ya goin...'

He threw something and I caught it mid-flight. Fifties wrapped in a band. He sat smiling. Rolled it in my palm and threw it back.

'No thanks, man. I'm cool til we're back on track.'

He picked it up and left it beside a pile in the corner. 'Always the hothead, Charlie boy. I'm lookin forward to some good times.'

'See ya in a week.'

He peeled off another eighth, said: 'Good times, Charlie, boy. Good things.'

We'd gotten €35,000 from the Post-office job. Not a lot. There'd been a fuck up somewhere. All the cash hadn't been delivered the night before. It was en route as we'd been robbing the place. Give it a name. The papers said the fortunate mistake had inspired a security overhaul for every branch in the country. Fuck it. With the split and all the drink and less robbing, I had about six grand left. It was under the floorboards at my house. That was my fund to make a start in Galway.

We hooked up at the safe house a week later. It was night and it was cold. The door fell closed and we were enveloped in darkness. Kramer lit a stolen candle, then we sparked smokes from the flame. Stale air and nicotine and a sense of ceremony. There was lots of shit piled up that we'd never sold. DVD players, laptops and stereos. Crates of booze and cartons of cigarettes. One time, Kramer took a couple of bowls coz they had designs and he figured they were antique. We saw them in a shop the next day at a fiver for two. They were still sitting in the corner like a bad joke.

'Man, we got a lotta gear here.'

I dragged hard, said: 'Damn right. Fence gonna take it all?'

'Yeah. He wants all the electric shit. Has a client in Claremorris.'

'What about the booze?'

'Pub uptown, always tryna beat the brewery. Think we can swing him round. We keep the smokes and jewellery, flog 'em in the city. Use 'em as barter to make a start and maybe get in with the locals. Fuck the rest of it.'

'Where's the fence now?'

'He's meetin us at the top of the road in an hour.'

'What's he givin us?'

'Straight grand.'

'What's it worth?'

'Bout one-five. That's a damn good stereo and the TV's got a plasma screen.'

'Good deal for him.'

'Discount for bulk buyin. I ain't used him before either.'

'Where's the regular guy?'

'Sent down for six months. Tried sellin smoke to an undercover agent.'

We got working. Felt like we were moving house or something. Guess we were. An hour later. Head of the road. Moon out. Carrying electrical goods in a wheelbarrow. Shoes wet from the grass. He was waiting. Big guy. Hands in his pockets. Muffled up. Black heavy coat. Needed a shave and a haircut. Breath like sour milk and a smoke hanging to the left of his mouth. He stood against the car. A rusty red Cortina. Boot open. Kramer said. 'Like the wheels.'

'Tryna to keep a low profile.'

Kramer smoked, said: 'Sticks out like a fuckin spacecraft.'

'Ain't been pulled yet.'

'Better not be tonight either.'

'Don't worry. I know the back roads.'

'Got the grade?'

'Under that stone beside ye.'

Looked down, rock beside the gate, borrowed from the wall. I didn't like the guy, said: 'Good thing you ain't awkward.'

'It's the way I work.'

Kramer was suspicious. 'Check it out, Charlie.'

The guy said: 'Wait til I'm gone. Someone might be watchin.'

'Watchin what? You fuckin us over?'

He shrugged. I pulled back the stone. A thin roll of money underneath. I did the count. 'Sixteen fifties. Two hundred short, chief.'

He tried shock and surprise, said: 'Count it again.'

Came up with the same.

'I coulda sworn there was a grand.'

I said: 'Just as well we checked.'

'Yeah. It is.'

Kramer threw his smoke away, said: 'So where the fuck is the rest?'

'Jesus, I don't think I have it. That's all I brought with me.' Patted his pockets, stupid look on his face. 'Hang on and I'll check the car.'

He walked back and Kramer took out his Stanley. 'He comes back with anythin less, I'm havin his fuckin throat.'

We watched him ruffling round the back seat. He came back looking baffled. Shaking his head, real forgetful. 'I don't know, lads. I musta left it somewhere. Can I meet ye with it later?'

I hit him the first blow and Kramer was on him from behind, arm round the throat and bringing him down. He was on the ground in a second. Nose bleeding, looking afraid. 'Lads, lads, lads! What the fuck is this?'

Kramer drew some blood from his neck. 'The last ten seconds you're gonna live.'

He broke straight away, musta been the sting of the blade. 'Alright, alright. Hang on, hang on. I know where it is now. I know. Just please, relax. It's just a mix-up.'

I gave him a boot to the ribs. He squealed. 'Stop! I told ye, I have the money!'

'Where the fuck is it?'

'My back pocket. My fuckin back pocket.'

He was wearing the pants of an old suit. Took a few seconds to wedge the wallet out. Found a thick wad of notes inside. Counted it. Kicked him in the teeth. Delighted to feel them break, said: 'Greedy fuck. Got at least another grand in here.'

He groaned like a sorry coward. Kramer squeezed his windpipe hard, whispered: 'Think you can fuck me? Think I'm a bitch? Like you can screw me outta dough? Thought I'd let it go coz I'm leavin town? Huh?' He cut him again and I figured it was lights out. He'd never killed anyone before. There was never any reason. But I figured it wasn't in him either, until now. 'Wanna die?'

He dug deeper and the fence started weeping. His voice all warped and sounding drunk and retarded. 'Please, Kramer, stop. I wanted an edge. Just like you and everyone else.'

Kramer looked up at me, then pulled back the blade before it hit the vein and we set to work. Beat him unconscious. Maybe we killed him. Who knows? It felt good, justified. After, we left the all gear but I threw a rock through the screen of the plasma television.

Back at the hut. We packed up the movables. I started on a bottle of wine. It tasted good, like hate. Drank from the neck. Steady shake in the hands. Feeling cranked. Intoxicated. We sparked smokes. Took a seat on a couple of crates. It was like we'd passed a big test. I said: 'First time a fence tried that.'

'Yeah. Can't trust anyone now.'

'Gonna be worse in the city.'

'We'll just have to adapt.'

'Think you woulda cut him?'

'If he held out anymore with the money, yeah.'

'We got an extra grand from the prick, too.'

'Fuckin loser.'

'You think we're gonna make it up there?'

'Yeah, or die tryin. How you feelin?'

'Like it's a goldmine.'

'You have to be ready for whatever comes down the line, too.'

'Fuck it. Give it a name.'

'I mean it, man. Things could get tough.'

'Like you said: Or die tryin.'

He looked around, said: 'That's it. Let's get the fuck outta here.'

Bootlegged the booze uptown and kept a couple of bottles for myself. Went to my gaff and the fuzz were waiting across the road. Expected another shoe search. Stared them down. Thought they'd jump out and approach, but they were just staking me out.

Packed my bags and called Kramer. He was getting wheels. I told him bout the cops and we decided to meet at the back of the house.

I went and got my hidden grade from under the floor. It was wet and dusty but still good. He arrived five minutes later. Leather seats, good tunebox and a golden dashboard. Threw my jacket in the back and lit a stolen smoke. Took out my songs, Manic Street Preachers: *Elvis Impersonator*. Opened a bottle of vodka. Saluted and said: 'Let's do it.'

The Smirnoff tasted slick, wild and warm. Exit Ballinrobe.

CHAPTER NINE

The contact's name was Simon. He was a real city kid. Black leather jacket and greased red hair. Blue jeans and acne. Classy looking watch and liked to flash his cash. He set us up with a pad in Lydon Court, just off the city centre. Standard bedrooms and a balcony. Saw myself chilling there with a smoke and a few beers. It all felt good.

Spent the first week on the piss; hanging around the Spanish Arch and making connections. The city crews were always looking for numbers and Simon introduced us to a lotta people. They all took his word that we were solid. Kramer settled in real easy, like a creature in his natural habitat. He had the way of the streets down in no time.

Started with some small-time work. Wallets and bags, small shops, shit like that. It was child's play, but we needed to test the water, get the run of the place. Simon became a regular at the flat and we learned all our stats from him. He worked for a guy called Max, big into dealing coke. One night, over a flagon, he asked: 'So you guys lookin for some real work?'

Kramer answered. 'Oh, yeah.'

'My employer needs a favour. Small risk. Good profit. Wants reliable people.'

Intervened, said: 'If it's drugs, forget about it. Too fuckin messy.'

Kramer gave me a look of death, said: 'We're interested.'

Simon noted the tension and continued: 'Max knows a trainer in the racin business. Last week he was told this horse was gonna come through. so he laid on some heavy grade. Told his associates to do the same.'

'What happened?'

'Came fourth.'

'Tough luck for Max.'

'Aye, fate and all that shit. Thing is, he heard the bookie was told the horse would lose.'

I said: 'What?'

'Think about it. Bookie puts up the odds, trainer goes back to Max, tells him he heard of a great place to lay a bet downtown — best in Galway. Max takes his word, tells a few people about the tip. Everybody figures they're ridin on a winner. Horse loses, trainer and bookie clean up.'

Kramer was pensive, said: 'Where do we come into this?'

'Trainer's head was found in a bin yesterday, but the bookie's been braggin round town.'

'And?'

'Max lost twenty grand on the race. His friends lost ten altogether. He gets it back, the rest is for whoever does the job.'

'There'll be fuck all left after that.'

Simon's eyes glinted. 'Grand National comin up. Think it could be good for about eighty large.'

I said: 'We could do the job ourselves and save the dough.'

'Max has the inside track — security codes, times, that kinda shit. He could do it himself.'

'Why doesn't he then?'

'Coz I advised him to give ye a start. Do it right and there'll be more. Fuck it up and it's your own fall.'

'When?'

'Bout two weeks.'

Kramer said: 'And we keep everythin after thirty large?'

'That's the idea. It's a principle thing.'

Drank more, smoked more. Simon gave us the run on the city. How Max was self-made. Came up alone and took over the drug scene. Known for being ruthless. Simon knew he had an eager audience and was glad to explain the mechanics of the operation.

Max was a supplier, and dealt mainly in cocaine. He was at the top of the ladder and was always separated from the street by at least two degrees. He bought huge quantities from the people Simon called the boatmen. Then he had it shipped to a secret location and broken down into smaller, more manageable packages.

This is where the middlemen came in.

Ultimately, these guys acted as a fence for the snow. They come and, depending on local demand, buy as much as they need. In turn, the middleman acts as a second-hand supplier and meets the needs of the dealers. The dealers can then either sell it directly, or have someone push it for them on the street. But Max prefers things done in private.

Local legend: On the way up, Max took over a local dealer's turf. He had a girl at the time. She was on the way home and was pulled into a car. Given a few slaps and a message for Max: next time we'll kill her.

Max wasn't happy. Decided it was time to make an example of someone. The dealer's head was posted to his parents a week later. First class, registered, had to be signed for. The act was to become his trademark. After that his operation grew. A couple of wars cleaned up the riff-raff and shit got organised. He was the first one in the city to give the business a sense of structure. Before that, it was everyone for themselves. Now it was like a booming black economy.

I opened another flagon. He continued.

There was always a negotiator to deal with the middlemen. Very few people knew Max personally and this was the way he cultivated the empire. Simon was the eyes and ears on the street. The wildcard that transcended all levels. When a shipment came to the docks, Simon was there to oversee everything and make sure it got to the next phase without any problems. If a dealer, or a middleman, tried to undercut Max, or set up his own operation, it was Simon's job to know and report it back. As a perk, he was allowed make some dough on the side and keep an infinite supply of his own.

'The drug squad are gettin real fuckin sniffy these days, too. You can't just hire anyone now. We need guys with brains that won't crack with a few slaps. The fuzz got everythin from dogs to buggin devices.'

'Many get caught?'

'Once in a while. Maybe a dealer gets coked up and sells to the wrong client. Or maybe he's bein watched and the D.S. decide to bust him.'

'Anyone ever squeal?'

'Fuck no. They stay quiet and their family gets looked after. They say a word, the whole bloodline gets wiped. Simple.'

We took it all in. Simon was really enjoying himself. I asked: 'You think the D.S. will ever catch up?'

'Never. Max is too smart. Someone even said he has an agent on the payroll — but no-one knows for sure.'

Kramer stood up, walked to the window, said: 'I wanna meet him.'

Simon laughed, pushed out his palm. 'Hold your horses, cowboy. He needs to know you're solid before he'll even look at ya. This guy can be one paranoid motherfucker and the coke don't help.'

'When then?'

'Do the job, do it well, and I'll see what I can do.'

Kramer replied as if he hadn't said anything: 'We'll deliver the money personally.'

Simon's cool edge faltered. 'Like I said, I'll see what I can do.'

'Tell him that's the way it is. Or no deal.'

Simon looked at me, like I could add sense. I just shrugged.

'Well at least it can't be said ye ain't got balls, lads.' Polished his booze and stood to leave. 'I gotta go. I'll call ye one of the days and we'll make some plans.'

Shook his hand and said: 'Cheers, Simon. See ya then.'

He left. I opened a can of cider, asked: 'Why you wanna meet Max so bad?'

'I wanna see if he is who Simon says he is.'

'Can't take his word?'

He lit a smoke. Frowned against the flame of the lighter. Dragged hard, exhaled. 'No. Maybe he's tellin the truth, but I ain't kickin thirty grand up to a fairytale neither.'

'I reckon you freaked him out.'

'Way to have him.'

I swigged hard, offered him a can.

He went. 'Jesus Christ, man, you still fuckin drinkin?'

'Yeah, what about it?'

'Lookin for a holiday in Hope House?'

'What's the fuckin problem?'

'You been on the piss all evenin. Ain't seen you sober since we got here.'

Took a defiant drink, said: 'Think he'll meet us?

'Depends on a good job.'

'You trust Simon?'

'Yeah. He's just a pawn, doin what he's told.'

'I just don't want my head in a box.'

'Then stay sober, keep your eyes open and watch my fuckin back.'

'What's this hang-up with booze?'

'You're a fuckin spacer when you're drinkin, Charlie. I need a wingman up here, not a pisshead.'

'If the shit goes down, I'll be there.'

'You fuckin better be. There's a lot comin up and I need ya sharp.'

'I'm good for it. What're ya plannin?'

'Get the bookies done and work it from there.'

'You always think further ahead than one job.'

'We gotta be careful for a while, then we can make bigger plans.'He threw his cigarette out the window and left.

I finished the can and started on a bottle of vodka.

CHAPTER TEN

Interior. Night. Stolen Car. Simon drove. Kramer and I did the raid. Had codes and keys. Went smooth, lifted sixty-three large. We were out in fifteen minutes. Back in action. Good grade and no hitches. Went to the flat and did the count. Got the thirty ready for Max and split the rest. Had more anxiety about him than doing the fuckin job. Simon left the bag on the ground and took a wrap from his pocket. Looked my way, asked: 'Got an ATM card?'

I knew what he was getting at, asked: 'What for?'

'Need to cut up some snow.'

'Then do it in your own fuckin pad.'

'Chill, Charlie. What's with the attitude?'

Kramer intervened with: 'Just do it, Charlie.'

'I ain't condonin that shit.'

'Condone con fuckin moan.'

He gave him one. We watched Simon chop up a line, bout the length of a pencil. Kramer was mesmerised. Simon hoovered it up, said: 'Let's go meet the boss.'

Simon was the pilot. Buzzing on the coke. He drove aggressive. Took corners hard. Got to Westside car park and he swung around. Breeze came in and I swigged for warmth. Still had the shakes. Coming down from the job. Gearing up to meet Max. I asked: 'This is it?'

'Yeah. He's on the way.'

Five minutes later the BMW arrived. Sleek like a water snake. Parked parallel. Simon said: 'We sit in the back, make the drop and leave. Ok?' Kramer said nothing, so he looked back at me: 'Ok?'

'Yeah. Ok.'

Outside the car. Cold. Quiet. Gave a scan around. No eyes watching. Slid into the big man's wheels. Simon first, then me and then Kramer.

Almost dark. Streetlight coming through the windshield. Kat at the wheel, looking ahead. Another guy in the passenger seat. All quiet. Simon was agitated and broke the silence. 'Hey Max, these are the guys.'

Voice came from the left, not the guy driving, said: 'I figured.'

Silence again. Kramer had the cash. Max asked: 'Was it a success?'

Simon looked at the bag, said: 'Yeah.'

'Good. You got my grade?'

'Yeah...Kramer has it.'

Max lit a smoke and opened the window. The night air swirled in. I swigged some more. Caught his reflection. Pale face, flat hair and dark, almost black, eyes. He went. 'So what did you want, Kramer?'

The driver sparked up too. I joined in with a Benson. Max said: 'I don't remember givin you permission to smoke?'

Kramer, defiant, said: 'We're givin you thirty grand for the pleasure.'

Driver turned, looked African, round head. Max continued: 'You didn't answer my question.'

'Heard that you were hard, not to be fucked with. Wanted to see for myself.'

'You didn't believe Simon?'

'Thirty large is a lot to put on a man's word.'

Max smiled. 'Sure is. You convinced now?'

'No.'

Driver looked back, said: 'That can be solved.'

Max didn't flinch, said: 'It's ok, Jules. Relax.' Turned to us. 'Simon was right about you, Kramer. You got balls, it's admirable.'

'Glad you think so.'

'But say anythin like that again and I'll be feedin your testicles to your friend here.'

'Whatever. Your dough's here. We gotta go.'

'All there, Simon?'

'Yeah, Max. Counted it myself.'

'Pass it to me.'

Kramer let go with reluctance. Max looked in. 'Looks good. Nice job, gentlemen. That'll be all.'

We left Simon there. Drove back. I polished the Bucky and started on a bottle of J.D. Got to the bridge, breezed through the lights at a cool eighty. Kramer was fuming, said: 'Prick.'

I took and swig and asked: 'You reckon he's hardcore?'

'He's a prick.'

'Think you coulda pissed him off.'

'Hope I fuckin did, smarmy little bastard.'

'Had a big geyser with him.'

'Hirin the fuckin refugees, coz they'll work for nothin.'

'At least we made an impression.'

'Bollocks. He didn't even say thanks. Last job I'll ever do for anyone else.'

Burned the car in Dyke Road and walked back to the flat.

Simon called round the next day. Looking sheepish, said: 'Well, men?'

'Well, Simon?'

'Max ain't too happy bout last night, but he'll let it go coz I told him you were ok.'

Kramer said: 'Fuck him.'

Simon, taken aback, said: 'That's not a healthy attitude, man.'

'Life's too short for healthy.'

'Max specialises in torture.'

'What's your point?'

'I know where you're comin from. He doesn't look like much, but he's a real...'

'He has it easy. Maybe he was hungry once. Way I see it, his image of himself is too pumped up with coke.'

'What are you tryna say?'

'I'm sayin he couldn't stand a challenge.'

Simon blinked, went: 'What?'

I seen the grade you make and you're only small-time.'

'I can't be hearin this.'

I asked: 'What the fuck you talkin bout, Kramer?'

He looked right at me, said: 'The coke. I'm gonna give Max a run. Make some contacts, some moves. See if he's got the muscle you're all talkin about.'

Simon, sounding frantic, said: 'Kramer, that's the stupidest thing I've ever heard.'

'That's what they told him, too. And look at him now. He's number one....'

'You got nothin to back it up, man. No connections, no crew, nothin.'

'I got you.'

'Me?'

'You.'

'That's insane.'

'I know you want more. You're a fast mover and you're not gonna take shit from him forever.'

'You think I'll go against Max?'

'I know you want the power. Don't tell me you're seriously kickin up all you earn, that you're not takin somethin for yourself.'

'There's a difference between a skim and coup d'état. I could get killed just for havin this conversation.'

'Might as well make it worth your while then. I know you got some sideline contacts. Ones that Max doesn't know about.'

'I'll never betray him.'

'Yeah you will. You already have, in your heart. I can see it. It's only a matter of time before you do somethin stupid and get killed. He's watchin out for it too. Mark my words, you're in a lose-lose.'

'If I tell him what you're sayin, you'll both be dead by mornin.'

'Tell him then. But you'll miss your chance.'

'Of what?'

'To be a big player. To command the situation. You'll have respect, and that's somethin you can't buy. You earn it.'

He tried to laugh, went: 'Earn what? You're some cowboy, Kramer. You and your bitch, Charlie. Thinkin you can take on the city. You'll be washed up in the weir by the weekend.'

'So be it. But there'll be no cunt sayin I didn't do things my way. But you. You might live another twenty years. Makin money for pricks with big cars they don't deserve, while you do all the work on the street and then die like a fuckin nobody.'

'Fuck you.'

He slammed the door on the way out. Kramer sat smug on the chair. I opened a bottle of Powers, said: 'I don't like bein called your bitch.'

'He just needs time.'

'I thought this drugs shit was over.'

'It's the future, Charlie.'

'Maybe yours, but not mine.'

'Think about it.'

'There's nothin to think about.'

'Then starve.'

'There's plenty of cash in what we do.'

'Then do it. This is the way I'm goin. I decided last night. It's the only way to make it up here.'

'I disagree.'

'It's all profit. Money's money, no matter how you make it.'

'I ain't goin down that road.'

'But you'll piss your life away instead?'

'Go fuck yourself.'

'You don't like it, then get the fuck out.'

His temper was going. Lethal, ready to attack. I took another swig of the whiskey, said: 'You were thinkin this since we left the Robe.'

'You're with me or you're not. This is bigger than principles.'

'That's where you're wrong. That's where you lost sight of the whole fuckin thing.'

He walked towards the door, said: 'Yeah, you're a real hero when you're robbin old folks in shops and puttin diabetics in wheelchairs. Then you get a moral fuckin crisis when it comes to chemicals.'

He left before I had a chance to answer.

I woke up that night on the couch. Kramer was talking to some kat bout calling over and not being followed and shit. He hung up and dialled again. Quick, to the point, said: 'We're good. 10 o'clock.'

Click.

He looked down, saw my lids open, said: 'There's people comin in an hour. I suggest you get your shit together, or disappear.'

He went into the kitchen and made more calls. My head felt like there was an iceberg trying to break through. Stomach feeling dodgy. Lit a smoke. Mouth all dry, like I'd been licking sandpaper. Eyes watering and the shakes on the horizon. Hadn't eaten in days. One can of Bud left. Opened it. Cut the windpipe, temporary quench of thirst. Placed smelled like a bad couch. Think it was the bad couch. Table with empty bottles. Upturned ashtray on the ground. Butts pressed into the fabric.

Needed to change the threads. Scent of sweat and piss. Teeth felt like they were wearing a jacket. A bloody, brown jacket. Mind all jumpy. Everything loud. Everything silent. Everything loud. Wanted another blackout. Threw on my coat. Kramer was still talking on the blower. I took the stairs down; used the wall for support.

Got outside. Door shut behind me. There was a smell of something burning. Tyres maybe. Saw Roches. Waited for a gap in the traffic. Stumbled across. Fell in, looked for the offy. Few looks from civilians. Aggression building. Demented need taking over. Found heaven, saw: Jack Daniels, Powers, Gin, Sambuca, Vodka. Opted for the Russian. Two bottles. Went to purchase. Hand shaky. Chick behind the counter. Young, cute. Black uniform. Blonde hair, sweet smile. Customer friendly. She scanned it, said: '€39.99 please.'

Exterior. Eyre Square. Night. The vodka tasted like a beautiful dawn. An escape from a terrible darkness. Took a seat on a bench by the fountain. It was damp and cold. Guy sat down, worse stink than me, a smell of old damp clothes and lost hope. He had stubble. No teeth. Grey and greasy hair. Long coat, shoes ripped open. Gloves that reached the tips of his fingers. A group of shirts walked passed. Hugo Boss and tight haircuts and arrogance. The guy gave me a nudge, said: 'Hearts of stone. They've all got hearts of fuckin stone.'

I agreed and drank. He watched me swallow. I figured he was out. I had half a bottle left and the second stashed inside my coat. Handed the half over, said: 'Happy Christmas.'

He looked at it. At me. Then took it and drank. I opened the other and we saluted. Took out my smokes and we sparked together. Asked him: 'What's your story?'

He took in the booze and dragged heavy. Didn't let the smoke out and dragged again. There was blood in his ear. Fuzz cruised by. Slowed, observed, and kept going. He said: 'Used to be a bank manager.'

Spotted Simon coming round the corner, headed for the flat. Figured he musta taken Kramer's bait.

And so it begins.

Shot the shit some more with the homeless guy. Said his name was Peter. Polished the smokes and booze. There was a family somewhere. And an incommunicable past. Left him a hundred from my wad and split. Got back to the flat. Met Kramer and Simon, doing a count on the kitchen table. Stack of cash and some coke chopped and ready to go. Simon gave the heads up. Kramer said nothing, just snorted a line like he was proving something.

Time passed.

People started calling. Kramer and Simon undercut Max on price and nearly everybody made the switch. It started with some regulars. Yuppies looking for a fix before a night on the town. A fix and one for the road. Max had had a monopoly for years and exploited the city's lack of choice. Now Kramer was selling for half and still making a healthy profit.

Word spread and there were people over all the time. Simon was the organisational wing of the operation. Same job, different master. Kramer was the brains and the muscle. He was out on the street. Making connections and recruiting sub-dealers. Soon he had a hardcore crew together, guys to collect debts and ensure swift deals.

I came home one night and it was just Simon. I sat on the couch with a can of Linden Village. He was busy cutting up gear and getting ready for the evening's clientele. He looked over, saw the cider, said: 'Hey man, want a real hit?'

Declined with a shake of the head.

'How come you never go for somethin better, Charlie? That shit'll kill ya.'

He snorted a line, threw his head back and sniffed. Rubbed his nose. I said: 'No. *That* shit'll kill ya. What ya gonna do when Max finds out?'

'Go to war.'

'War?'

'Turf war. May the best man win.'

'Thought you were afraid of him, like he was invincible?'

'Yeah, I was.'

'Was?'

'Kramer's a real bear, like Max used to be. I think he's hungrier. My money's on him.'

He had another hit and the doorbell rang. Simon answered, brought the coke in to the kitchen and set to work.

Soon, the drop in business was enough for Max to smell a rat. He sent out feelers and got back the stats. Heard Simon was playing both sides. Exit peace. Galway had a new coke war.

I was so damn drunk, I didn't care.

CHAPTER ELEVEN

The first casualty was a dealer working for Kramer. He was found on College Road. No eyes, ears, or tongue. Simon said it was another Max trademark. Kramer heard about it, took a line and grunted. He came back that night and they discussed retaliation. Simon knew the ins and outs of their operation. It meant Max could be hit where he was weak. They took out a middleman the next evening. Bust in, took the coke and grade, set him alight and left him in Eyre Square. It was a real swift kickback. Told Max that Kramer had an edge. That he was prepared to go just as far.

There were more clients coming up to the flat all the time. Simon became a hermit at the house and people always had to call before they were allowed enter. He knew how important it was to Max that all double-crossers received a slow and painful execution. A much larger police presence appeared on the streets too and there was an air of guerrilla war everywhere. Kramer switched his routines regularly and hired more middlemen. He was proving a real warlord, evolved straight to a big player. He spent the nights prowling the city in different cars. Phone ready for word of an attack. Dozens of people on the lookout for talk of moves against him.

Things reached a new low when an ex-customer of Max was found face down in a pool of his own blood. Kramer retaliated by throwing a rival dealer from the roof of The Meryick Hotel.

Two nights later, I woke up on the couch and there were six to eight hoods standing round taking stats from Kramer. They all had a serious edge, like they were at a funeral. Picked up the vibes. They were making plans for an all-out assault. Element of surprise and shit like that. List on the table, supplied by Simon — all he knew. They were goin for Blitzkrieg. Nothing small that Max could take a hit on. They were all armed, dressed in black, doing lines. A real crew of criminal militants.

They went out that night and burned all they could find that had anything to do with Max. Took out safe houses, dealers, cars, warehouses. The gem was the shipment routine. Max was due a six-month drop that night and they decided to intercept. It was beautiful. They came home with an animal amount of coke and a sense of victory. Kramer was hailed as the new number one and everyone figured Max was gonna fold. The next day there was a call from Jules: the enemy wanted a sit down.

When I heard about the meeting, I was interested. It sounded like something from a gangster movie. I was drinking at the flat when Kramer told me I was going with him. I asked: 'What the fuck would I go for?'

'Max says he has shit to say, and he wants you to hear it, too.'

'No way, man. That makes me part of it. I got enough problems.'

'Charlie, we're leavin in five minutes. I told them you're neutral and they understand. Get your shit together.'

I took a drink, said: 'Sounds like a hit.'

'I thought of that. The place is covered. It's just a sit-down. Hurry the fuck up.'

Full-time drinking. Robberies. Sit-downs with drug lords. How the fuck does this happen? I swallowed the thought with some vodka and pulled myself off the couch. Kramer did a line in the kitchen and took the car keys off the table. Simon came outta the bathroom, zipping up, eyes wide. Looked at me and asked: 'Ready?'

It took place in Bohermore. Place called O'Grady's. Deal was: Max and Jules were to meet Kramer, Simon and myself. Got there. Spotted their BMW outside. Guy sat at the wheel, looking like a real Sicilian, all sported up in sunglasses.

Interior. Pub. Dark. Stench of bleach. Tension. Max and Jules at a table, leather jackets and drinking coffee and looking sombre. Low ambience, real pulp fiction style. Picture Jules, arms folded like a fuckin cliché. Max opened with: 'Drink, gentlemen?'

The other two declined. I wanted to say: 'Triple vodka with a dash of orange. Slap it in a pint glass with cubes and a lemon.' Instead, I said: 'No, thanks.'

Max signalled the barman for more coffee. They waited, like a ritual, until he was gone. Jules stared at Simon, like an angry bulldog. Max said: 'Well?'

We left the talking to Kramer. 'Well what?'

'Well, how we gonna sort out this mess?'

'One of us is goin outta business. And right now, the odds are on you.'

'Don't flatter yourself.'

'Don't get cocky. You had it made, and then you got kicked in the teeth. Now you're come beggin to me.'

'Not necessarily.'

'What do you want?'

'A truce.'

'Didn't hear these calls when you were attackin my clients.'

'All's fair in love and war.'

'Get to the point.'

'I have a D.S. agent on my payroll.'

'Bollocks. Don't believe ya, and if I did, what's it matter?'

'Coz he could use a good bust. Needs one now and then to keep the heat off me.'

'So?'

'You know what I'm sayin.'

'You wanna threaten me with the law?'

'Not threaten. We can use it to our advantage. My suppliers are gettin nervy bout the war. I have to feed them some good news.'

'Feed them Jules. He's a fat ass. He'll keep them full for a while.'

Jules pulled a stupid face, like he'd just sat on something wet. He got up, all aggressive. Max tamed him with a touch and continued. 'Kramer, you got this far with aggression, but now it's time to start usin your head.'

'*You're* givin me advice?'

'The deal is this: we make a truce, cease the attacks on each others' business. You take the east side. I take the west. We don't cross over. Clients make up their own mind about who they wanna buy from. I'll supply somethin for the agent. We all get rich quicker. It makes good sense.'

'There ain't anythin in it for me. I'm doin fine. And what's this got to do with Charlie?'

'I told my agent nothin. But there's somethin I thought the three of you would like to hear. He asked if I knew anythin bout a job in a bookies. Three guys, fit your description. Walked with about sixty three K. He's got friends on the case and they'd like a lead. I can fix it so he stops lookin, turns a blind eye. On the other hand I can give a nod in your direction. I don't like havin to deal like this men, it's not my style. But I'll do what it takes to make things run smooth.'

'Bullshit. You woulda used him already.'

· 'I wanted to win this war myself. We need to get the business back in shape. That's what's most important. Our suppliers don't need to hear about big busts and informants. Things are bad enough as it is.'

Kramer, remaining calm, said: 'That's all you called us here to say?"

'We gotta fix the prices.'

'Back up to yours? Not a fuckin chance.'

'I'm willin to meet you half-way. Think about it, when you lowered the price, it became more affordable. More clients, more cash. Now that they're hooked, we put it back up. It'll be still be affordable, but there'll be more profit.'

'And we end the war here?'

'Competition's good for business, but not war. We're both losin.'

'What about the agent?'

'I'll take care of him.'

'Any heat and we're straight back to the guns.'

'It won't be my fault.'

'If it is, you'll know about it.'

'Let's keep reasonable, Kramer.'

'Fuck reason. One bit of heat, and it's bullet time.'

'One other thing, I need a new shipment. After your stunt the other night, the word on the Atlantic is that Galway's a real cowboy town.'

'It ain't far off.'

'Less ships are willin to risk a war-time drop. I'm takin in a stash at the docks soon. Bring your crew and we'll split it, as a sign of faith. It'll show the boat crews that we're all patched up too.'

'Sounds like a set-up.'

'Simon knows I'm a man of my word.'

Simon nodded. Kramer said: 'I'll think about it. Is that it?'

'For now. Let's just try and avoid war in the future. It's easier this way.'

'One move outta line, agent or not, I'll fuckin kill ya.'

Jules cut in, said: 'Hey, enough threats.'

'And you can go fuck a monkey.'

Max stood up, stern, said: 'Gentlemen, a pleasure doin business.'

No one said goodbye.

Interior. Flat. An hour later. We took in the meeting with some Marlboro and alcohol. I opened a can of cider, asked: 'So what's the verdict?'

Simon smoked, thought and said: 'Hard to know. He's big into that business shit, but he's a snake too. True bout his word though. Never known him to break it.'

Kramer was sitting with his elbows folded across the back of a chair, said: 'We coulda taken him out right there. Fuck that agent.'

'Wouldn't make sense, man,' said Simon. 'Like wavin a flag to the D.S. We ain't got no ties with them. They'd be on us like dogs. Let Max deal with them, and we can get rich in the dark.'

I swigged, asked: 'How long's he got this guy on his payroll?'

'First heard it bout two years ago. He really hung us with that bookies shit.'

Kramer smoked: 'We could take the heat. It always dies down after a while.'

We drank in silence, watching the smoke float between us. Simon broke it: 'Way I figure: give it a chance. Balance the price and the suppliers. Get everything in line, then when the time is right…'

Kramer said: 'Move in and swoop the whole gig together.'

'Exactly.'

'I like your thinkin.'

'Learned it from Max.'

'Guess he's thinkin the same way.'

'I'd put money on it.'

'We'll keep him sweet until we know he's gonna pounce, then beat him to it.'

Simon stubbed his smoke into an overflowing ashtray on the ground, said: 'That just might be the way to go. Right, I gotta a run to do.'

'You good for that drop at the docks?'

'Yeah. He won't make a move yet, needs to lure us into a false sense of security. It's a charade for the boatmen too.'

'I hear ya. Call me later.'

Exit Simon. Kramer turned to me, asked: 'What d'ya think?'

Slugged, said: 'Simon's right, Max is a snake.'

'It's all venom in this game.'

'You think it's only a matter of time?'

'Aye, the town ain't big enough. Peace makes sense now, but it won't forever.'

I took a drink, said: 'He's smart too. Dumb fucks don't make it that big.'

'I still think we shoulda taken him out.'

'Might work better this way.'

'Him and his fuckin agent.'

Few months went by. The truce held, but it was fragile. Tension building all the time. Kramer sharpened his game even more. He was like a wolf. Took no chances at all. Different cars, more middlemen, no talking on the phone. Me and him got frosty too. Like we couldn't stand each other. Me drinking. Him dealing. Nothing about what we came to Galway to do. Both of us knew it would come to blows eventually. Wasn't like we were gonna sit down and discuss our feelings. Fuck, there's only one way people like us know how to communicate. I was asleep on the couch when I heard his voice. Aggressive. Full of threats. Thought there was someone else in the room, then realised he was talking to me. I asked: 'What's your problem, man?'

'State of the fuckin place.'

Grains on the table, rubbing his nose. I stretched and got up. 'Are you not supposed to be out dealin or somethin?'

'Winos make me sick.'

'Hey, fuck you, coke boy.'

'Don't start me, Charlie.'

'I was unconscious til you came in.'

He lit a smoke and paced the room. Looked out the window, like there might be someone wanting a fight. Decided I was offended. Pulled a can of Dutch Gold from under the couch and said: 'Wanker.'

He was on me like a lion. Roaring. Saliva, teeth, screams. Pulled me off the couch, against the wall. His forehead connected twice with my nose. Flashflash. Took a left to the jaw and then a right. Tried to swing one back and he went low. Uppercut in the gut, two hands on the back of my coat. Pulled it over my head. Knees connected with my mouth. More stars. Ears all muffled. Sound of short serious breathing. Took another two rights to the head and hit the deck hard. He got me with two kicks to the ribs. Winded, rolled over. He pulled a fire extinguisher from the wall, towered over me, roared: 'I'll fuckin kill ya!'

Figured he was serious and stayed dumb. Could be curtains for Charlie, cracked skull, intensive care, coma, all that. He threw it aside. It knocked over the table and crashed in the corner. Then he took the Stanley from his hoof and came from behind. Arm around my neck, couldn't breath. Felt the steel against my throat, cold and sharp.

'I'll fuckin slit right through, you hear me?'

'Fuck you.'

'Right fuckin through!'

He yanked. I had memories of the fence, said: 'Alright, alright. Chill the fuck out.'

He whacked my head off the ground, said: 'Get outta here, you fuckin disgust me.'

I stood up, badly bruised, blood flowing. He threw the blade on the ground and turned his back. There was a ringing inside my head like a very loud tuning fork. Went to the bathroom and checked out my reflection. Looked like I'd barely escaped a bomb blast. I stopped at the door on the way out, said: 'Congratulations, Kramer. Congratulations.'

And I left.

Chapter Twelve

Exterior. Shop Street. Friday evening. Church bells in the distance. Leonard Cohen in my head - *The Stranger Song*. Dark coming, looking forward to the night. I hadn't been home in weeks. Knew nothing about the war situation, cept there was a helluva lot more cops around. No words with Kramer since the scrap. Got to The Quays. Folks outside, smoking, drinking, singing. Was on the prowl for some easy money. Went inside and found a nice leather wallet on a table by the back. Everyone up dancing, no one watching the grade. Enter Charlie, stage left.

Exit by the front door.

Walked passed The Spanish Arch towards Nestors and on to Father Griffin Road. A squad car flew past. Sirens wailing. High speed. I stood at the playground and counted. Kat had a loada notes and a whole lotta cards and shit. I went back for more. Took a left towards Cross Street. Queue for the ATM outside the Bank of Ireland. Had an easy catch. Jailbait with a short skirt, clicking up the road, dropped her purse. Stopped to do my shoelace and picked it up. Another fifty. Half hour's work — who needs coke? Gave it a rest. Bought a bottle of Smirnoff in The Vineyard and drank it on the window outside. It was getting damn cold.

Time to start thinking bout a place to stay. It was that time of the night. Was making ok grade, hand to mouth with a bit left over. Decided to walk to the Arch. Got there and sat on the ground against a bench. Took in my vodka and listened to the roar of the river. There was a light wind and a distant smell of weed. Spaced out. Half-asleep. Night brought a full moon. Another siren wailed in the distance.

Then something moved beside me. Two figures, blocked out the light. Angle to the right: Max in a leather jacket, calm and smoking. Behind him stood Jules. I drank vodka and played it cool. Stayed looking at the water and waited for him to open.

'Well, Charlie?'

'Well, Max?'

'You look afraid.'

'I never had anythin to do with you and Kramer's problems.'

Took in the whiff of his cigarette, smelled like Camel. Jules stood like an anvil behind me. I drank more. The bench was sticking into my back. Max was perched on his knees, then he sat down. 'I hear you two haven't been seein eye to eye lately.'

'Why're havin this conversation?'

'I want to give you a chance.'

'To do what?'

'Kramer and Simon will be dead in an hour.'

'So you gonna make your move?'

'He left me no choice, and I could never forgive Simon anyway.'

'You still haven't answered my question.'

'Why are we havin this conversation?'

'Yeah.'

'Because I want it done tonight, before they reach the docks. We're doin another pick-up together and the boatmen are edgy enough without gunfire.'

'Then do it.'

'I need to know his route. Kramer sends three to four cars out every time he leaves the house. I wanna know which one's his.'

'Call him and ask him.'

'That's what you're gonna do.'

'I don't think so.'

'Do it and I'll let you live. I know you're no part of his operation, but it's a respect thing. If you don't sell out on Kramer then I have to assume you're against me.'

'Assume all you like.'

'You'll die with them, Charlie.'

I took a drink, said: 'We'll see.'

'Jules.'

Heard a shuffle and felt the barrel against the back of my head. Everything got louder, even the click of the hammer inside. Thought about all sortsa things, like making a run for it. But the gun had me paralysed.

Max threw a card in my direction: 'Dial this number. You have an hour.'

And they were gone.

It took me the rest of the bottle to reassemble. I considered my options. Self-preservation was screaming. I calmed down, took out my phone and dialled. He answered right away.

'Speak.'

'Max approached me. Wants to know your wheels. He's makin his move tonight.'

Silence.

Click.

Next I rang Max. He answered with: 'Which car?'

'Go fuck yourself.'

'That's very stupid, Cha —'

Click.

Threw the phone down. Had Pink Floyd in the head: *The Great Gig in the Sky*. Rain came small, cold and refreshing. Things were going to get bad and I wanted to lay low. I wasn't neutral anymore. Left in search of somewhere to hide out for a while. Came round by Mainguard Street. Cops had a kat against the wall. Bright lights from the squad cars flashing. The cops were forceful, using handcuffs. Car door open. They shoved him in and took away. Saw him through the window, recognised him from the flat. One of Kramer's pushers.

I bought another bottle of vodka and opened it outside The Cellar. It tasted like the last one of the night — enough to knock me out til the morning. Decided to sleep in a car park off Bowling Green. Work everything else out in the morning. Stood up to make my way there when the BMW screeched to halt. I knew what it meant the second I heard the tyres. Jules drove. Max rode shotgun, with a shotgun. It had all the beauty of gangland. My brain told me to move but I felt locked to the ground. The window came down slowly and I made eye contact with the two barrels. Max stared from inside, said: 'You had your chance, Charlie.'

I winced, expecting the blast. Someone pulled me to the ground. The bottle broke and cut my hand. The shot rang out, loud as a bomb, and smashed the pub window. Some glass rained down. Most of it went inside. The guy kept me pinned to the ground as the tyres screamed away. All went quiet and we stood up. He was a typical heavy at a door. Asked me 'You alright?'

'Yeah, think so.'

He looked at my hand. It was pumping blood. Laceration across my palm. He said: 'Better get that looked at. I don't know what the fuck is goin on in this city tonight.'

'What d'ya mean?'

I felt like I was under water. He assessed the broken window, like a goalkeeper looking towards the far the end of the pitch. Two guards in yellow jackets appeared outta nowhere. Real young and aggressive. Pushed me against the wall. One of them called over the bouncer, asked: 'What happened here? Did this man cause any trouble?'

'No. I was just gonna ask him to move because he was drinkin at the window.'

'And who were they shootin at?'

'Him, I think. Or the pub. Coulda been some prick we refused to let in or somethin.'

One pig went to disperse the crowd and deal with the traffic. The other looked at me and said: 'People have any reason to shoot you?'

'Not that I know of.'

'What's your name?'

A familiar voice said: 'Charlie?'

We both looked over. It was Peter, the guy I'd shared my vodka with in the square. He was armed with wine and concern. The cop turned back to me and asked: 'You homeless?'

'Only when the hostels won't take me.'

'Into drugs?'

'Does vodka count?'

Peter took a drink, said: "D'ye not have any real work for doin other than botherin the likes of us?'

The cop patted me down. The bouncer said: 'To be honest, I think they were just tryin to get at the pub.'

The fuzz radio squawked. Looking for back-up. The cop pushed me against the wall again, said: 'I see you one more time tonight and you're going straight to the cell, you hear me?'

Peter said: 'Hey, take it easy.'

I nodded, said: 'No problem.'

He let me loose, took the bouncer's details and told him he'd be back. I walked to Eyre Square with Peter. He had a slow pace, and the drink didn't help. We took a seat on the steps outside the Bank of Ireland. He gave me a slug of the wine and slurred: 'Fuckin cops.'

Had a bout of post-trauma. The fact that I was nearly killed hit me with enormous clarity. That, and what about my vodka? Got up and stretched. Felt rusty and slow, like a hinge that needed to be oiled. My hand bled more and started to ache. Got the whiff of the fast food from Supermacs. My body protested again, like I'd fallen down a stairs. Lit a smoke and tried to collect myself. Wheeze in the lungs, cold cheeks and damp hair. Offered one to Peter; he accepted. I thanked him for his help with the cops and he suggested a house party. Figured it was best to stay outta the limelight. What was I doing still walking around?

It was a joint on Prospect Hill. No panes in the windows. Barely a door and a couch that looked nothing like a couch any more. It smelled of rot and urine. Full moon gave us light from the outside, compensated for the lack of electricity. Things with too many legs walked casually across the floor. I'd bought a couple more bottles on the way. Broke the seal and drank. My hand continued to bleed. There were other homeless upstairs. They sang and drank and threatened each other, but left us alone. All looked sorta like Peter, maybe like me too, I didn't know anymore.

Peter talked. It was his daughters' twenty-first. He was celebrating. He'd gone to the pub and they told him to fuck off.

Later, when we were tanked, he fell asleep on a chair that made gangrene look healthy. Things were quiet upstairs too. They'd peaked an hour before, then muttered some more and fell silent. I contemplated the darkness. Listening to the world outside, feeling like I was on the sidelines. Thought about Max and the double barrel and how long I'd last before they tried again.

Soon enough, I ran outta drink. Couldn't sleep. Didn't want to. Got sick of sitting around. Got up and went back to the flat for all sorts of reasons, mostly drunk ones that I can't remember. Think I needed to take sides, stand with Kramer, fuck it, if they were trying to kill me, mighta as well go down shooting.

On the way, a fire engine screamed passed. And there was smoke in the air everywhere. Distant sounds of tires screeching, the loud report of a gunshot, cops on foot patrol at all the corners.

I got back to Lydon Court. Something went through me as I stood in the hallway, a shiver, like an Arctic chill, or a host of people I might have been. Heard the commotion as I neared the top of the stairs. There was shouting, real police talk, just like in the movies. Listened at the door. Heard shit like: *under arrest… with intent to supply.* I slipped in unheard. Got to the living room. Saw the back of a uniform, yelling at Simon to stay down. I went and got my steel bat. Simon looked up, made eye contact and winked. I took out the first agent with a swoop to the back of the skull.

Another guy was handcuffing Kramer on the ground. He looked up, saw me and took a dive in my direction. Caught me with a rugby hold and winded me against the door. Kramer was behind him in a second. Picked up the bat and knocked him out. We stood panting and a blast of sirens erupted outside. Simon looked over my shoulder and said: 'Watch your house!'

Turned. Cops flooded down the corridor, all torches and batons. They were on me straightaway. Cuffs and threats. Had me belly down, arms twisted behind my back. Kramer and Simon escaped through the balcony. Something hit me from behind and I went unconscious.

Chapter Thirteen

Woke up in a cell. Hard bed, bars. Body weak, eyes felt like stones. Ache in the back of my head, like it was open. Thought back, just the highlights, gave me a wave, knew I was in deep.

Felt like morning. It *was* morning. Stretched out, palm scraped across a cold wall. Still in my clothes. Bunk bed. Looked up, saw the bulge coming down. Wanted a smoke. All my shit was gone. No wallet, no grade, no sticks. The cage door swung open, real Hollywood style. Two kats came in, looking stern. Would've expected square heads and glasses. Instead, got weather-beaten and greasy hair. Craters in the face, yellow teeth, jackets creased. One turned to the other, said: 'That him?'

He gave him the nod, real mute and solemn effect. Disapproving looks. I felt like a dog that had pissed on a new carpet. 'What's your name, son?'

'Charlie.'

'Charlie who?'

'I could tell ya but I'd have to kill ya.'

'Cut the smartass shit. You have any idea of the trouble you're in?'

'I gotta feelin you're gonna spell it out.'

'You're going down, son, all the fuckin way.'

He jingled some coins. The mute coughed and looked around the place, like he was in a fuckin museum or something. There was a stir in the bunk above, then a voice all croaked, said: 'Hey, folks, think ya can shut the fuck up? Guy tryna get some kip around here.'

The mute spoke. 'Shut up, Oscar. Speak when you're spoken to.'

'Fuck you.'

They turned on me again. 'Get up, Charlie. We're gonna ask you some questions.'

'Now?'

'Someone will escort you out in ten minutes. Be ready.'

I rolled outta the scratcher, already dressed. Agents left a smell of sweat lingering in the air. Floor was grey, insects running around. Took a slash in a bowl in the corner. Sat back and waited. Oscar moved again, groaned: 'What're you in for?'

'Dropped an agent.'

'My kinda man.'

'Think I'm fucked?'

'You ain't gonna get praise.'

'Need a plan. A plan and a smoke.'

'Can help you with the smoke.'

He sat up, legs hanging over the edge, and pulled out a twenty pack of Major. He was older than me, maybe mid-twenties. Greasy hair, stubble, dark eyes, gaunt. Black threads. He asked: 'Why'd you clock him?'

'Moment's madness — arrestin my mates.'

'Clean sheet besides?'

'Far as I know.'

'They have a warrant?'

'Never asked.'

'Ask. These fucks can be real fuckin Nazis.'

'Who're ya tellin?'

'They get your friends?'

'Dunno.'

'What they want 'em for?'

'Dealin.'

'Smoke?'

'Powder.'

'Max?'

'Kramer.'

'Heard of him.'

'All good I'm sure.'

'That Max was a prick. Bout time he got smoked.'

Instrumental.

Then I said: 'Smoked?'

'Yeah, he's a thing of the past.'

'How d'you know?'

'Last night, on the way down here, it came over the radio. Thought the pigs were gonna spark the champagne.'

'Who pulled the trigger?'

'Couldn't tell ya. All I know's a lotta shit went down, and now you're here. I figure these fucks are desperate — raidin places, not gettin warrants. You gamble they didn't have one, and you came home, found kats bustin up your house, acted in self-defence.'

'And if they got the papers?'

'Say nada; they gotta prove shit. Like there was gear at your gaff, like you're a dealer. Did the pig die?'

'Dunno. Doubt it.'

'You're small fry, Charlie; they want the big players. They'll ask you to roll.'

'How you know I'm small fry?'

'Coz I got my ear to the ground, I know what's happenin on the street. If you were in deep, I'd've heard about it.'

Uniform walked in, said: 'No cigarettes please.'

'Get a real job, fuckhead.'

'Shut up, Oscar.'

Looked at me, said: 'Charlie?'

'Yeah.'

'You're wanted in the interrogation room.'

Stubbed my smoke on the ground and stood to go. Oscar said: 'Don't let them lean on ya, Charlie. They're worse crooks that you and me will ever be.'

Cop followed me up a long corridor. Place smelled like a swimming pool. Squeaky tiles and large strong doors. Bright lights and lotsa kats in suits with folders and pencils, talking to blonde chicks with glasses.

Place was decorated with printers, shredders and water-coolers. Phones ringing, fans flying, plants growing. Like a fuckin mental hospital. Came to a thick door that said: Interrogation Room.

Interior. Table. Iron legs and plastic cups. Low lighting. Seats like deckchairs. Empty besides. Cold. Expected a mirror on the wall, like it was one of those joints with kats observing my movements, sipping caffeine and having a good old laugh at Charlie. But no reflection, not even a window. Four blank walls, another water cooler in the corner. Sat down, uncomfortable. Felt shaky, jerking. Horrors were coming, tried to forget about it. Door swung open. Guy from the cell, not the mute.

'Charlie!' He was real chirpy like we hadn't seen each other in years: 'We meet again. My name is Geoffrey.'

'Alright, Geoff. Any chance of a smoke?'

'None. Now, what're you prepared to tell us?'

'Fuck all.'

'You can do better than that, Charlie. We got you hung by the balls. You're talking about a long stretch.'

'Great, need the holiday.'

'You do realise that hitting an officer is a very serious offence?'

'Really? Well hell, chief, do they pay you well for tellin people shit like that?'

He lost his cheerful edge, said: 'I get paid to put pricks like you in jail, and I don't do it for the money. I think you and your dealer friends are the scum of the earth.'

'Scum of the earth? That's a real kick in the teeth, Geoff. You really hurt my feelins.'

'Listen, Charlie. You're up before a judge in the morning and, unless you roll over on your friends, I can guarantee you a stay in Mountjoy jail.'

'We gettin a train or a bus?'

'You're leaving me no choice.'

'You got plenty of options.'

'I don't think so.'

'Sure ya do. First off, you gotta show me a warrant. Think you can haul me in here all Hitler style and lean on me till I crack?'

'We're always on the right side of the law.'

'You sure?'

'Hundred and ten per cent.'

'No dirty cops on the force?'

'Don't be ridiculous.'

'Not what I hear.'

'The hell are you talking about?'

'Try Max — him and his fuckin empire. You sure he hadn't any of you monkeys under his thumb?'

'Max is dead.'

'Shit happens.'

'We want Kramer, Charlie. With Max outta the picture, we know he's the big fish.'

'So go get him.'

'That's where you come in.'

'I'll never roll on Kramer.'

He shifted a bit in the chair. Opened up his folder, let a slight whistle through his teeth, acted like he was scanning the pages. 'They left you there. They ran out of the building while you were lying unconscious on the floor.' 'Fair play to them.'

'It's not very loyal, is it?'

'All you pigs are the same — always tryna play people against each other. Forget about it, it ain't happenin.'

'We'll see.'

He got up to leave, buttoned his jacket: 'If you change your mind about talking, call one of the officers outside your cell and I'll be waiting. If not, I'll see you in court.'

'Don't forget your warrant now.'

'We won't.'

He left and I was escorted back. The place smelled like sawdust. I sat on the bed. It creaked. Oscar threw me a cig, asked: 'You give em hell?'

'Yeah, fuck 'em.'

'What they doin ya for?'

'Dunno. They never said. Just kept leanin.'

'Don't know themselves. Just makin ya paranoid.'

'Be paranoid enough when the horrors set in.'

I lay back and slept. The whole shit deal spun round in my head. Time in the Joy held no appeal. I woke up with the shakes an hour later. I had never cross-referenced the word addiction with alcohol. Whatever the fuck people said, I never put them together. It was just booze.

Now I had cold sweats and a constricted chest. Falling dreams and my stomach was wrangled in knots. I pulled the blanket over my head and tried to sleep. Started seeing shit. Hearing voices, like Kramer's, Simon's, those bastard fuckin cops. Mind went blank, didn't know where I was, came back again. Wanted to puke. My right hand started shaking outta control and it became shit hard to breathe.

Mouth dry, I wanted water. Tossed and turned. Prayed for time to pass. Couldn't close my eyes, kept spiralling, room spinning. Figured a pint would do, just the one. And a whisky, double; make it a triple. Gin, off the head, fuck the tonic. vodka. Vodkavodkavodka. Gimme the fire. Get it in the fuckin system. Jerkshakejerk. Got up, stumbled to the basin, took in some water. Coughed, drank more. No edge. Tried to puke, didn't happen. Thought my intestines were gonna come through my mouth. Blood, the colour of tar, leaked out. Cramps. My body screamed: gimme a fuckin drink. Felt Oscar staring at the back of my head. Hung on to the bowl; more blood. Room was like an outta control funfair ride. Everything went black, like going under water. I came up again, saw the world through blurry eyes. System felt like I'd just swallowed battery acid. Image: spottedleakingrotten liver. Stood again and swayed back to the bed. Layered in sweat, gasping for air. Heard Oscar get off his bunk and I thought of all the bad jail films I'd ever seen.

'Charlie boy, you're in a fuckin mess. You been on the H?'

I coughed some more and a lump of dark red phlegm fell on the covers.

'Jesus man, your blood is almost black.'

I couldn't talk. He was asking me questions but I just kept blacking out. He caught my hand to stop it going crazy, but couldn't hold it. I sensed him back away and go to the door. At the same moment, something ruptured — like a grenade went off inside me.

I tried to shout but couldn't stop heaving.

Everything went: conscious/unconscious/conscious/unconscious. Felt like I was leaking somewhere. Spasmspasm. No control. Unconscious/conscious, saw a uniform. Cops ugly face staring down, asking stupid questions like: 'What's wrong with him?'

My body screeched, like the brakes of an out of control train, and I came to an excruciating halt, face down in a pillow of blood, under the gaze of an unqualified audience, wanting nothing but to die, or to have a drink — or whichever came first.

CHAPTER FOURTEEN

' With this patient we had changes in the regional blood flow of the brain, especially hypoperfusion in the frontal cortex and the right temporal region. Some research suggests that this rebound activity might be related to augmentation of brain excitation from hyperactivity of the NMDA receptor system.'

'And this is what caused the seizure?'

'Yes, seizures are sometimes attributed to pre-existing brain damage, but can be triggered by the abrupt cessation of long-term alcohol abuse and dependence. A typical symptom is a severe overactivity of the ANS. Some respiratory problems, along with increased temperature, are not uncommon.'

'Will he return to normal?'

'Yes and no. Yes, with the help of some long acting drugs, such as Chlormethiazole – otherwise known as Hameneverin – he will recover from the process of withdrawal. However, his addiction has resulted in some irreversible damage to his kidney and liver.'

'And what are the effects?'

'Ultimately, he will be able to function like everybody else; his body has the capacity to filter the regular fluids and poisons of his system. His liver was incapable of that process when he arrived and he was close to death. Any extra demand, such as the resumption of alcohol intake, will result in an immediate overdose and is likely to be fatal.'

'Is that common?'

'Sometimes, but this is what some might call rock bottom, which it literally is. There is no choice now but for the patient to admit that a problem exists and seek appropriate help.'

'How long will he be here?'

'The most dangerous period of the withdrawal is the first five days. But it can continue for weeks. Our unit will monitor him until the majority of physical discomfort is over. After that, he will be transferred to a clinic, where he will receive therapy and possibly some anti-depressant medication.'

'Anti-depressants?'

'Recovery from alcohol addiction is often marked with decreased feelings of self-worth, lessened libido, nervousness and insomnia. Long term abuse leaves very little room to develop other interests. An alcoholic rarely has routines, social circles or sleep patterns that are not dependent on consumption. The crater that exists after cessation is often difficult to fill. This, as one can imagine, results in a strong drive to resume drinking.'

'And how likely is it that he will drink again?'

'Difficult to say. His response to treatment will give a better indication, but there are external factors which can trigger a relapse.'

'Such as?'

'Inability to cope with stress, to deal with life and its obstacles without needing a crutch; a negative response to treatment, and of course, the lack of a desire to stop.'

'Can he feel any discomfort right now?'

'It's unlikely. The medication is quite potent, but we do need to be conscious of his delicate liver. He may experience some confusion and restlessness as we decrease the dosage.'

CHAPTER FIFTEEN

White ceiling, bright lights. Softer bed. Thought it was another cell. Pain in my stomach like I'd been ripped open. Found out later it was coz I'd been ripped open. Doctor standing on my right.

'Are you conscious, Charlie? Can you hear me?'

'Loud and clear.'

'It looks like you were a very lucky young man.'

'What the hell happened — I get shot or somethin?'

'No, you should be ok. You're starting to recover and, provided you stay away from alcohol...'

'How long I been in here?'

'Three days.'

'Ain't I supposed to be in court?'

'Yes, but then you nearly died.'

'But...'

A nurse came along, young, fresh as a rose, said: 'He's awake?'

'Yes, but he needs rest. Continue his medication for another forty-eight hours.'

She smiled and left, shoes squeaking on the floor. Smell of disinfectant and bad food. A television blared somewhere in the distance. Doc inspected my pupils, then took my pulse and blood pressure. I asked: 'The fuzz still wanna send me to the Joy?'

'That's none of my business.'

He put on his stethoscope and started on my chest. Finished and wrote something on the chart. Scribbled his name on the bottom and started on an old guy with bad lungs.

World felt like a Rubix Cube. Shit hard to figure out. Wave of panic came with images of court. Mad for a drink. Made plans to hit the booze as soon I got the chance.

Lids got heavy and I slept. Woke up to Geoff's face. Stern, serious. Head was whoozy — wasn't sure if I was dreaming. Asked him: 'Are you real?'

'I'm not here to joke, Charlie.'

'I ain't jokin.'

'You knew there was a corrupt agent on the force.'

'So did half the fuckin city. What's your point?'

'He was the one who raided your flat.'

'I figured. That's you fucked, then.'

'For now, but you'll be back. Kids like you always come back.'

'Not me, chief.' Gave him a wink and called: 'Nurse!'

'Don't forget there were two officers injured. We have to follow procedure. The court's in three days and you could be looking at time. We could make that disappear, but only if you're prepared to provide us with the information we need.'

'Sure ya could, but I'm doin just fine here, buddy, doin just fine.'

Nurse came over, different from the last time. Ugly, big arms. A matron.

'What's all this shouting?'

'Just lookin for my fix, doll. Fresh out of pills.'

She looked at the chart, scowled. 'You're not due for another two hours. Stop disturbing the other patients!'

She squeaked away. I looked at Geoff and shrugged. He said: 'I'll see you in court.'

Thought: I wish he'd stop saying that.

Later, shit was getting serious. No sign of the hit, no nurses either. Wanted a beer. Chills and a tremor kicked in. Looked for my threads; figured they were locked up. Thought about the window. Got up. Legs weak. Unsteady. Pulled the drip from my vein. Walked, found a cupboard, tried it. Nothing. Went up the corridor, saw EXIT. Made my way towards it. Folks incoming, spaced. Kats in wheelchairs. Everything smelled like porridge. Felt like I was walking on wooden stumps. Got to an electric door, it opened with a smile. Felt the night breeze. Heard the trees, a car drove past with a swoosh. Cold. Nightshirt open.

No shoes. Bout to make the leap for mankind when her vocals tickled my spine.

'Charlie! What the hell do you think you're doing?'

Turned, it was the ugly nurse. Felt like I'd just been caught stealing, said: 'Bathroom?'

She pursed the lips, hand on hip, pointed with the other. 'Back there.'

Shrugged and retraced. Got to the bed after, enveloped in panic, like I just saw the wings fall off the side of the plane. The pretty one finally arrived. Cute and fulla smiles, plastic cup of water and two pills. Took them in the paw. They were round and pale yellow. She said: 'They're to help with your withdrawal.'

Knocked 'em back.

'There we go. Now you just rest, Charlie, and call me if you need anything, ok?'

My body calmed, said: 'All's I need is one look at you and I'm knocked out already.'

Sat back and let them kick in. Submerged. Didn't dream.

Woke up to a new face. Sitting patient at the bedside. Temperature high. My first thought was to get a drink.

'Hello, Charlie.'

Beard, red jumper, slacks. Young and looked like a teacher.

'What's your game, another doc?'

'Not exactly. My name is Brian.'

'Corrupt cop?'

'Juvenile Liaison Officer.'

'J.L.O.?'

'That's correct.'

'Got any medication?'

'Fraid not. I'm here to assess your situation before we bring a case to the judge.'

'My situation ain't too good.'

'I can see that. Has it occurred to you that you have an alcohol problem, Charlie?'

'Did the detox give it away?'

'You're not here by choice.'

'You got that fuckin right.'

'I want to help you.'

'Get whiskey?'

'Get sober, and stay out of prison.'

'You a shrink as well?'

'Not exactly.'

'Nurse!'

She didn't come. He was still talking. 'You have to go to court soon. If I can convince the judge that you're serious about going dry, then he should be lenient.'

He had my attention, I said: 'Sweet.'

'You need to be genuine.'

'Don't worry, coach. I'm the real thing. You got my word.'

'I'll have a chat with the doctors and come back tomorrow. You think about your future.'

'Will do, Brian.'

Time passes with the beat of a man's heart. Your liver's one of the organs that doesn't grow back, like brain tissue. That's why when you spend a shitload of time on booze; you get more than a fuckin hangover. The doctors said I was lucky, but slipped the word *irreparable* somewhere in between. They used words like: *overdose, cirrhosis, motor neuron disease, jaundice, degeneration of the cerebellum.* One more bender and it's curtains for Charlie. Liver's on the last stand. Can't take the pressure. Stomach rotted to shit. Lining gone, ulcers. Been self-digesting for weeks. Same as a man on hunger strike. Mouth sores, bad teeth and gums, like a sailor with no fruit. Last of the poison about to leave the system, scorched earth in my body. Confused hunger — alcohol or pills? The prospect of eternity rises up to meet me. Asks: what the fuck are you gonna do now, Charlie? There's no terror like the unknown, except the unknown forever. And in the past there's peace.

Here now it's all: show him hell and call it side affects. Bring him to meetings, group counselling. Ask him to discuss his feelings. Label him as aggressive and angry, without respect for authority. Give him aptitude tests, make him tick boxes and solve puzzles. Finish and make a report. Highly intelligent but nonresponsive to therapy. He can't be fixed here. Recommendation: re-entry to society, to be observed by his J.L.O. for a period of twelve months. He's taking up space. Get him the fuck out. Case closed.

CHAPTER SIXTEEN

Brian was a genius. He got the case postponed for medical reasons and I spent a month in the hospital. Went through the mill and dried out. Court came after. Real charade. Couple of kats from the D.S. in the corner. Whispering, passing notes and shit. Few honchos with wigs, papers and briefcases. Place was real commotion. Top cop up the front, taking oaths and seating the rats. Stenographer. Journalists scribbling. Families at the back, all grim and arms folded. Judge was in a shit mood. Shot down a few hot lawyers on technicalities. Lots of young heads representing themselves. Caught drunk on the street, abused the cops, hauled in, fined five hundred and bound to the peace.

I was all suited up and groomed. Good to go. Brian had a couple of folders and held his head high, watching everything. They called my name. We took a seat near the front. Some kats in uniforms were sworn in. Didn't see the guy I'd clocked. Statements were read out. Near the end, old Geoff arrived and went through our chat in the interrogation room. Had it all written down. Sounded accurate. The bits I could remember. Judge asked a few questions, it came through about the corrupt agent. Brian was called. He was unbreakable. Had the law down. Talked about my age, the warrant thing, self-defence. Flirted with words like conspiracy and cover-up.

I was called forward. Walked up. Heart doing overtime. Looked at Brian. He gave me a signal to say: get your hands outta your pockets. I did. Joined them, like I was at mass. Judge said: 'You've been dry for a month now. Do you think you can keep it that way?'

'Yes, sir.'

'You realise what a serious offence it is to hit a police officer?'

'Yes, sir.'

'If not for the report of the Juvenile Liaison Officer, I would have no qualms about sending you to prison. There were no drugs in your system at the time of the incident. Are things going to stay that way?'

'Yes, sir.'

Looked at Brian. Figured we had it in the bag. The judge addressed the court. Spoke of his disappointment in the D.S. and his concern for their future credibility. He turned in my direction to give the sentence. With the crooked cop, my age and my addiction, I got three years suspended and a warning: one more appearance and he wouldn't be lenient; I was getting the stretch and more, even if I was caught drinking. Wanted to do a Gerry Conlon: climb through the crowds, roar at the press and shit. But it was a non-event. The next case was called and we left.

Exterior. Outside the courthouse. Day.

Brian came with me, said: 'You just got a clear bill of health, legally and physically.'

'Can't step outta line for a year. One more session and I'm a dead man. Hardly clear but I'll accept.'

'You couldn't have asked for a better result, Charlie. Keep your nose clean and stay outta the pubs. Today's the beginning of the rest of your life.'

'Cheers, Brian. Guess I'll see ya round?'

I lit a smoke, offered him one. He refused, said: 'I'm your guardian angel for the next twelve months. Make sure you stay on track. You haven't seen the back of me by a long shot.'

'It's good to know, coach.'

'I have to go. I'll be giving you a call over the next few days.'

He started walking. I blew some smoke, said: 'Hey, Brian.'

'Yeah?'

'Preciate it.'

'Just don't disappoint me, Charlie.'

Stood in the vacuum. Taking in the freedom. Enter wiseguy, bout my age. He stood in my sun, asked: 'You got a light, man?'

Knew his style. He had the edge of kat connected. Figured he was up for something inside, but my antenna twitched. He sparked, stood and looked to the distance. Silence, figured I'd let him break it. He said: 'Kramer sends his regards, Charlie.'

'Isn't he the considerate motherfucker.'

'Appreciates that you didn't squeal.'

'It was nothin.'

'It was more than nothin, coz if you had…'

'You'd've had my head?'

He winked and smiled, said: 'He wants no hard feelins.'

'Tell him I'm goin my own way now. I want nothin to do with him, you, his whole fuckin crew. I'm goin solo.'

'I'll pass it on.' He stubbed out his smoke, said: 'Everyone knows what you did. You'll always have respect in this city.'

'You just tell him what I said.'

'He'll hear it. See ya round.'

He slithered away and I walked into the sunset. Crossed at the lights into Eglington Street. Destination unknown. Figured it was time to get a pad. Still had a roll of dough, thin but sufficient. Got a copy of *The Galway Advertiser*. Checked out a few places in Newcastle, Westside, Shantalla, the City Centre. All too small and overpriced. Found a place in Forster Court. Well kept, quiet, down the back. Good rent. Large room. Living with working folks. Appealed to me. Took it and moved in.

Time for the next part of the plan. Brian figured I should look for work, as part of my reintegration. Left and tried a few places in town. Nothing doing. All bars and factories and busy streets and windy evenings. Never really seen the place through sober eyes. Signs on clothes shop windows, phone shops and supermarkets. All part-time and bad pay. Kept an eye out for Peter, but never saw him. Wasn't sure what I'd do if I did. Wasn't worried bout meeting any of Kramer's crew. They were all night workers. In any case, I didn't care. Came home, despondent. Went to my room. Read the paper again. Felt new and old, outta place. Wasn't cut out for this conformity shit. Tried to sleep. Couldn't. Wide awake, heart beating. Time going slow, temptation creeping in. Flirting with the abyss. Lay on my back and lit a smoke. Just me and my thoughts.

Chapter Seventeen

B rian called two days later, asked: 'Get a place to stay?'
'Yeah, sorted.'
'Job?'
'Nothin yet. Goin on the hunt again today.'
'Think I might have something.'
'Oh yeah?'
'A library, at the university.'
Wanted to say: Seriously? Instead, said: 'Piss off.'
'That's gratitude.'
'I mean, seriously?'
'I don't have time to waste, Charlie. You can do it until you find something else.'
'Jeez I don't know, Brian. I mean, I never even read that much.'
'It's all about numbers, same as packets of soup. You just need to put the books in the right order.'
'I'll think about it.'
'I need an answer now. It's part-time, twenty hours a week. Will look great on your record.'
'When do I start?'
'Five this evening.'
'Fuck it.'
'That a *no*?'
'No.'
'That's a *yes*, then?'
'Yeah.'
'I'll tell them to expect you. Ask for John.'
Click.
Got out of the cot, checked the time. Noon. Had five hours to kill. Went to the pool hall, found a snooker table near the back. Enjoyed it better than pool: longer table, more tactics, bigger challenge. Spent the afternoon improving my game. Got to the college bout four. Thought I'd check out the joint. Kats all over

the place. Lots of bags, folders and mobile phones. Few heads
with bad accents. All drinking coffee, eating scones, spreading
jam — that kinda shit. Asked a blonde for directions to the
library. Found it. Went through the electric doors. Kat to the
left on a swivel chair. Going back and over like he was floating
on air. I said: 'I'm here bout the job?'

'Cleaner?'

'Stackin books.'

'Upstairs. Ask for John.'

Gave him the nod and walked through. Up to the first floor.
Place smelled like papyrus. Greeted by shelves of learning. Group
of chicks walked past, all blonde and sweet, books in hand,
surrounded by innocence and perfume. Man in a uniform came
along. Grey hair, black slacks and shoes. Saw me and walked
over, said: 'You look lost.'

'Lookin for a man called John.'

Extended his hand, said: 'At your service.'

Shook, said: 'Name's Charlie.'

'Ah, about the job?'

'Aye. Brian said...'

'I know. Brian told me you were coming. Come on, let's get
you acquainted.'

Turned down an aisle. Babe walked passed. My kinda
place. Libido gets thrashed when you're on the session. Sure,
inhibitions are down and you'd fuck a stray dog, but that's not
the point. Over time, you just lose the edge.

'We're gonna start you in the literature section.'

Shrugged, said: 'It's all the same to me.'

He spent an hour showing me the ropes with numbers,
stacking, shelves, genres, all the shit. Was all about order. He
left me to it, came back a while later. Impressed, raised the
eyebrows, said: 'You're a natural, Charlie.'

'Yeah, but it ain't exactly rocket science.'

He smiled, said: 'No, that's upstairs.'

Intercom blared. They wanted him at reception. He excused
himself, said I'd done enough for the evening, I was hired.

Stacked a few more and left.

It takes time for twenty hours a week to make you a fortune. It covered the rent, bit of food, but that was about it. After a while, I felt my bones creaking with the inactivity. My room became a chamber, another cell. I did nothing all day except hang out and wait for the evening, then back to the nighttime demons. I wanted hard work, something to tire me out. The world offered nothing but the shaking of heads and pseudo-sympathetic looks. Like they knew my kind and didn't want to let me in. Society getting its pound of flesh for all the times I fucked its over law abiding citizens.

I eventually found out the story of how Kramer won the war from an old newspaper at the house. It had all happened on the night I was arrested. The headline read: Gangland Murder Reaches Max. There was a picture of two bodies on the front and I had to read a whole lotta tabloid cliché until I got to the substance. With the article, and what I knew, I was able to piece together what had happened.

Seems Kramer gets off the phone from talking to me about Max making the move against him. He's coked up and the news sends him crazy, but he's thinking bout the advantage too. I call Max, buy another bottle of vodka, and stand outside The Cellar.

Kramer and Simon kidnap Max's most trusted middleman. They put a gun to his head and tell him to call Max and ask for an important meeting. It works. Max and Jules are on the way over in the BMW when they see me and figure they can't miss the opportunity. That's when the bouncer pulled me to the ground and they ended up shooting the window instead. After that, they musta gone straight to the middleman's place. The paper said Jules had been stabbed repeatedly and his teeth had been removed with pliers. Both his shoulders had been dislocated from the top down with a heavy blunt object and his spine was broken in two, most likely by the same weapon. His official cause of death was a gaping wound to the chest, caused by a blast from a sawn-off shotgun at close range.

Max had bee shot in both kneecaps and once through the anus. A screwdriver had been pushed through each earlobe and into his brain. His disfigurement was out-classed by what was later to become Kramer's trademark. His throat had been cut across the windpipe and his tongue pulled through the wound. The state pathologist had a quote at the end of the article. *'Gangland murder, especially of this type, has now reached epidemic proportions in this country.'*

When they got home, the corrupt agent was waiting. Max had played his last card, just before his meeting with the middleman. They were taking Kramer down when I arrived with my heroics.

Then, after I'd gotten arrested, Geoff investigated the whole thing and nailed the guy on Max's payroll. After that, they reviewed all the cases he'd ever worked on. Most of the animals Max had helped send down were released. It was like they'd unlocked the gates of hell, and all the free criminals thanked Kramer, then signed up to work for him.

CHAPTER EIGHTEEN

Interior. Bedroom. After work. Lay back, smoked and churned options. Getting late, feeling restless. Tunes on, long night ahead. My mind at war with two evils. Decided to hit the street. Threw on my jacket. Felt like getting back into uniform.

Exterior. Night. Shop Street. Someone once said that genius is the ability to go from A to C without considering B. I think it's the same with money. Wealth is the process of coming from having little money to having a lot, without having to work for it. I was robbing again an hour later.

Spent the night on the prowl, got a lot of action. Staked a few of the busy pubs, The King's Head, The Living Room, Bazaar. Clocked off around midnight. Got a can of coke in Mcdonagh's. Place smelled like grease and battered cod. Lots of fucks from the country outside. Coke tasted like tar. Cold, stuck to the roof of my mouth. Polished it, pushed through a few rednecks and threw it in the bin.

The night air tempted me with possibility. I was feeling good, like my favourite team had just won. Underlying thirst. Thought about the future. Time to get a distraction for the days. Knew I had something now for the nights, but wanted more routine. Grade in pocket, two solid hours of hardcore consumption. Fuck it, kept going. Kept the head down and faced for Forster Court. Got back. Felt alive, limber. Took out the dust and did the count. Sweet night, hit the five hundred mark. Notes felt warm against the fingers. Lay back and slept without incident.

Next day, hung out at the snooker hall until it was time for the library. Got there, met John. Same story, Literature section. Didn't need supervision. Went through the alphabet. Had the names down. Banville, Bruen, De Lillo, Dostoyevsky.

Nearly time for my break. Raining outside. Didn't fancy a wet smoke. Thought about hitting the canteen. Did it once before, read a bad paper, wanted something better. Took down a book, Banville, *The Book of Evidence*. Read the first page. It was loud with a fast edge. Got an image of hooves vibrating on the ground. Voice behind me, John's, said: 'Want your break, Charlie?'

Jumped and turned, felt like I'd been caught doing something wrong. He looked at my paws, took in the title and smiled. 'Big into Banville?'

Breezed the pages, said: 'Never read him. Never read much at all.'

'Never too late to start.'

I put it back, said: 'Guess not.'

Went to walk and he took the book back down, said: 'Want to borrow it?'

'Don't I need to be a student?'

'I can swing it, if you're serious...'

Brought it home. Great read. Got more Banville. Devoured it, then moved onto the other titles. Money started coming in too. Had a basic one sixty from the library dough, and made some tax-free on the street. Reading kept me going during the days. Found great tales and heroes, whole new worlds. Heading fast for a life of basic wants and simple needs. Coming close to finding peace, or at least as close as I was ever gonna get. Robbing was going well. Getting no heat. The past was becoming the past, leaving no trace on the now, at least nothing unmanageable. Brian called regularly, checking up, having a chat, making sure I was still being a good citizen. He came in one evening as I was just about to finish work. It's always good to see someone that has faith in you. He said: 'Heard you're doing well?'

'Yeah, keepin it real Brian, cheers. What about you?'

'Good, good...John tells me you've started reading?'

'Helps to kill time.'

'Good man.'

'You busy with the delinquents?'

He laughed, scratched the back of his head with a key, said: 'Kept going, Charlie, thanks. I'd like a chat when you're finished, if you have the time?'

Frowned, stacked a book, asked: 'Anythin up?'

'No, just a couple of things I think you should consider.'

'Be about ten minutes?'

'Ok, I'll wait downstairs.'

He left and I finished stacking. Met him in the staff room. Bright joint, white table with cup stains. Light brown wooden chairs and a tile floor, designed like a chessboard. Calendar on the wall with pictures of books. Fan in the corner beside a semi-live plant. Smokes left on the table, Marlboro with a lighter on top. Brian turned to boil the kettle. I stole the fags. He said: 'You'll have a clean sheet soon.'

'Don't get ya.'

'In six months time, your record's clear. The juvenile liaison programme will be over.'

'So I can fuck everythin up all over again?'

He didn't laugh, said: 'You can give some serious thought to your future.'

'One day at a time, chief, isn't that what they say?'

'Yes, but you'll have more flexibility. With a record, you are hindered from moving forward.'

'It's not like I ever wanted to go anywhere.'

'But now you can.'

'Where?'

He turned with two cups of tea, said: 'College.'

'College?'

'Yep.'

'Now you've really lost me.'

'You showed a huge intelligence in your assessment at the clinic.'

Wasn't sure if that required an answer, said nothing. He continued: 'It was one of the reasons the judge went easy on you.'

'And?'

We sipped. He opened a folder, said: 'The deadline for applications is coming up next month. I think you should apply.'

'I ain't done school since I was thirteen years old.'

'There's a thing called the Access program. I know the people down there and I can try to sort something out. Once you do a few aptitudes, I think you'll make it in.'

'What about my history?'

'Like I said, in six months time, your history's...history.'

'Hmm...'

'It's a chance.'

'What do I have to do?'

He took out some forms, said: 'Fill these out. Decide what course you'd like and I'll take care of the rest.'

'Yeah, but this ain't my scene, Brian. I don't have the head for it.'

'Try it. If you don't like, you can always walk away, but if you quit now, you can't always come back.'

Checked out the application. Inch thick. All sorts of shit about my situation. Thought about it, figured I had nothing to lose. It beat the snooker hall and gave me a licence to read all the time. 'What'll I study?'

'What's your favourite section upstairs?'

'Literature.'

'Try Arts.'

Scanned the list. Found it. Sipped tea, it was sweet on the tongue. The future opened. Brian watched, time to make a call. I shrugged, said: 'Let's do it.'

He smiled, said: 'That's a good move. Bring the application with you and call me when you're ready.'

'Thanks, Brian.'

'You deserve a chance, Charlie.'

Put it all in an envelope and left. I spent next few evenings watching the other students from the corner of my eye. It didn't look like a bad sorta life.

The next year involved three nights a week at the library and two in the Access programme. It was more of a challenge than I'd expected. It also filled part of the void left by the departure of alcohol from my life. Using my brain to its potential was something I'd never even considered, and now it was demanded of me. I nailed the exams and was accepted into Arts straight away.

Took on Philosophy, English, Sociology & Politics and History. Big reading lists. Had a lot of it down from my job in the bookhouse. Got big into Nietzsche and took in some Marx. Good theory but doomed to failure. Spent my time robbing and reading. College bait is good grade. Brian cut me loose too. His final words of advice were: 'You're on top now, Charlie. Stay ahead.'

Steered away from the drinking culture. Left me on the margins, but I kept up with the study. Did the exams, navigated my way to the final year. Shit got harder. Spent less time on the street. Papers talked about Kramer sometimes. He was like a shadow around the city, a ghost. Everybody knew of him, but nobody got close. Heard kats talking about coke, where to get it, who to know. Kids, innocent, all waiting to be roped in.

I usually took Fridays off, spent them in the college bar, shooting pool. Drank Mi-wadi, played for a fiver a game. Cleaned up. Couple of sharks around, but I was winning nine outta ten. Money piled up, started spending. Bought threads, stereo, books, that kinda shit. Things gradually translated into normal. It was like Alchemy. I'd changed lanes and I was doing ok.

One day, on the way to a lecture, I realised I'd spent my whole time in college alone. There were folks, like from the Access programme, who had similar stories, but I always did my own thing. I missed some things about the old days, especially the jobs. It wasn't just the money, it was the rush. I felt like a skydiver that had just been diagnosed with a heart condition. I was nostalgic about the life too, the association. I was no longer surrounded by people who thought the same way. All the conformity was destroying my soul. Give it a name, call it boredom. I wanted a change, something exciting, a challenge to keep my mind off self-destruction.

It was the last day of the semester and the lecture was on Marxist Economics, taught by a guy called McKenna. He was late. I took a seat near the front and everyone around me talked about the summer holidays. They were gonna do the States, Australia, inter-railing around Europe. I took out the course text and tried to ignore the babble. He bumbled in. Briefcase, sweat, coffee. Threw his phone, keys and wallet on the table and began the lecture.

I loved you as fully as I knew how to love,
and we were all innocent once.

Noel Duffy, *Hibiscus.*

Chapter Nineteen

The Gods give you what you want when they are trying to punish you. Woke up on El Niño's floor. Thought back on the night before. I told P.J I'd make the meeting, but I was really in two minds. It could be a trap: Kramer on a purge, wiping out all potential threats. If Joe was talking, he'd know the fuzz were on to me and he'd have to break the chain somewhere. On the other hand, a no-show meant something to hide. Decided I needed to think alone. Told El Niño I was going into town to shoot some marbles. She said she'd go check when her money was coming through.

The sun was out, the snooker hall offered a welcome peace. Three frames later I came up with a plan. I figured I'd move in with El Niño and meet Kramer. I gambled that he wouldn't kill me as long as he was convinced I wasn't going to talk to the police. I'd appeal to his sense of principle. Send all his rage to Joe. Tell him he owes me for the thing with the D.S. — like I was calling in a favour. And Malone could go fuck himself.

Interior. The house at Forster Court. Packed a bag. Brought some threads and tunes, zipped it up. Daylight coming through behind me, overcast. Heard footsteps on the neighbour's stairs. Checked out my collection of books. Didn't pack any, left them for the next guy that moved in.

Rang the landlord and told him I was a thing of the past. Dialled again and ordered a cab. It started to rain, light at first, then hardcore heavy, like the world was pissed off I was leaving. Fuck it, not much of a kat for omens. Lay on the bed, put on some Interpol, *Leif Erikson*. Took it in with a smoke. Damn good tune, perfect for a sense of departure. Dragged hard, lungs wheezed. Five-second movie of my time spent in the room. Mixed emotions. Like nostalgia, solitude and security. The place creaked, like it was getting ready to let me go. Tipped ash on the ground and rubbed it into the carpet. Threw on the jacket and gave it a moment. Heard bells in the distance. Exit Forster Court.

The front door squealed shut behind me. Bag on my shoulder. Houses on every side felt like eyes, all watching my moves. Had a neat layer of sweat across my back. Met the cab outside Tonerys. Sat in. Meter running. Driver was bout forty, belly and stubble. Talked about the city. Festivals: arts and oysters. Gambling: dogs and horses. Students: drink and houses.

Got to Laurel Park. Knocked. She answered, naked except for a towel. Seductively, she said: 'Step into my parlour.'

She walked through the hall with a curve. Naturally brown all over. I went to the living room, placed smelled like a Christmas tree.

Anxiety surfacing. Feeling stretched and caged. Heart beating irregular. Went upstairs to check the stash. The dead rat. The dust. The water tank. The money. It hadn't moved. Came down and she was in front of a mirror, brushing scraggled hair.

She opened: 'Thought I'd done a runner with your grade?'

'Just checkin. You do some research?'

'Yeah. I get my dollars next week.'

'What about flights?'

'Cash it all and fly the next day?'

'Sounds good. Where to first?'

'I wanna see London. Never been there. Do a month and work it from there.'

'You book anythin?'

'No, thought I'd wait for your opinion.'

'Suits me, whatever, never been anywhere anyway.'

'Where's all your stuff?'

'Kitchen.'

'One bag?'

'Yeah. I travel light. Tunes and threads — life's essentials.'

She finished with her hair and left the brush on the mantlepiece, said: 'How's the loose ends?'

'I have a meetin tomorrow night.'

'With the cops?'

'No, the others. It should buy enough time to get your money and split.'

'What if it doesn't?'

'We'll worry bout that when it happens.'

She frowned, lit a smoke and said: 'Wanna go book some flights?'

I climbed back up to the attic, got some grade and we left. Walked through the college, past the cathedral, and found an internet cafe on Shop Street. Went inside and booked two flights to London. She had a credit card and I gave her my fare from the Chartbusters stash. After, we stood outside, everything looked different, like the colour had changed. It had stopped raining. Her face in the Galway sun. She said: 'That's it, Charlie. It's official.'

'Aye, exit Galway.'

'I wanna go buy some new clothes for the different climates. You can come, or go back to the house.'

'Think I'll pass on both. I'll call you later.'

She left and I walked towards Woodquay. Saw him from the corner of my eye. He hadn't changed fuck all. Same hair and walk. Think it was even the same damn jacket. Cocky confidence, like he was untouchable. Anger swelled. He opened with: 'Well, Charles. Busy day?'

'Alright Simon, too hectic for small talk. What d'ya want?'

'Been a while.'

'Not long enough.'

'No hard feelins, eh?'

'Whatever.'

'Just makin sure you ain't forgot bout your appointment tomorrow night.'

'Got an office now has he? You his secretary?'

He took a smoke from behind his ear, lit it, said: 'This ain't any way to treat an old friend, Charles.'

'You should see how I am with the fucks I don't like.'

'Keep your friends close, but your enemies closer.'

'Jesus, Simon, that's fuckin profound. You come up with that all by yourself?'

He continued like I'd said nothing: 'Who's the chick?'

'She's called — none of your business.'

'She's got class buddy.'

'Unlike yourself.'

'Maybe you'll introduce me sometime?'

'Maybe you'll just piss off.'

'If you miss the meet tomorrow night, I might just introduce myself.'

'I'll have your red balls, Simon, and stuff 'em down your fuckin throat.'

'We'll see.'

He threw his smoke on the ground. Zipped up his jacket and put the collar real Elvis style, said: 'Good to see ya, Charlie.'

Exit Simon, enter murderous thoughts. Took the corner opposite the courthouse and Malone spotted me from across the road. He musta been in there on a case or something. He was over straightaway.

'Alright, Charlie?'

Thought: I'm the one that needs the fuckin office, said: 'Thought I wasn't gonna see you til next week.'

'Yeah, isn't this a stroke of luck?'

'In daylight, on a busy street, it's like a bullet in the fuckin head.'

'Joe's going into the Witness Protection Programme.'

'Good for Joe. I'll give him a month, tops.'

'I'm doing you a favour.'

'Then you're in the wrong fuckin job, Malone. You should be a fuckin undertaker.'

I walked. Took the scenic route home, hoping Simon hadn't spotted the chance meet with Sherlock. I called El Niño and asked if she thought anyone was following. She said she didn't think so but I told her to take the long way back to be sure. I went to the house and waited. She returned a couple of hours later. The conversation turned to this. 'You made me paranoid earlier, bout people following me. Everywhere I looked I thought someone was watching me.'

'Anyone approach you, ask you anythin weird, like even for directions or anythin?'

'No.'

'See anyone distinctive? Tall guy, red hair?'

'No, not that I noticed. Charlie, I don't like this any more. What the fuck is going on?'

'It's complicated.'

'Fuck complicated. I don't like being followed. I deserve to know and I got a feeling it's a helluva lot bigger than a stolen wallet.'

'I don't want to freak you out, that's all.'

'It's a bit late for that. Time to spill. I need more than *loose ends.*'

Thought about it, figured it was time to come clean, went: 'You ever hear of a guy called Kramer?'

'Kramer, as in *Kramer* Kramer.'

'Yeah, that's probably him.'

I told her everything — the old days, the jobs, Kramer's rise to power, my treatment. Then Chartbusters, Joe, Malone and my recent visit from Simon. I was selective with the gruesome parts. Afterwards, she was a bit pale and said: 'I've heard things, evil things about him...'

Played it down, said: 'That's just hype. I grew up with the guy; he's not that bad...'

'...and people that owe him money, their relatives get posted the body parts.'

'That's not gonna happen to us.'

'How can you be so sure?'

'Because I know him better than anyone.'

'What does that matter?'

'You just gotta trust me, babe. Take my word, nothin bad is gonna happen.'

'Tell me you know what you're doing, Charlie.'

'I got it under control.'

'I fuckin hope so. What do we do now, sit and wait?'

'I'm meetin him tomorrow. We'll work it out from there.'

CHAPTER TWENTY

There's no beating the hardcore damage you can do to your own body and feel good about it. Hell, I'd even drink weed killer if I thought it'd block out reality for a while. You get to my state and realise you've spent your life on the piss and picking pockets: it ain't pretty. But I don't know nothing else. Offer me ten euro today or a hundred in a year, I'll take the dough now. Who the fuck knows where I'll be in a year? Makes sense. But that all changes when you're thinking for two.

The meeting was in The Crescent in Salthill. I walked in and Kramer was having a game of sticks with Simon in an empty pool room at the back. He'd put on weight. His stomach hung beneath the cue and his jeans were wide and lagging. He was wearing dirty runners and a lot of jewellery, a far cry from the Hollywood godfathers. Simon was in the same clothes as the day before. They turned as I made my entry. I gave the heads up and walked to the bar.

Nice joint. Had an antique edge. Wooden chairs and a bright counter. Few lost ones at the bar, looking into timeless pints. Man and woman inside, retirement age. She came over, glassy eyes, dressed in white, smelling like newly washed sheets. Leaned across the wood to catch the vocals in her right ear.

'Cidona. Pint glass, lots of ice.'

She pulled back, head going up and down, muttered the request while she looked for it. Felt the eyes of Simon burn. Knew Kramer was playing indifference. Tapped the counter as she got the cubes. Mirror on the wall, saw my reflection, looking beat. Fuck it. She landed the glass with a rattle, said: '€2.75, please.'

I gave her the dough. She went to get the change. I took a slug of my bevvy, tasted the ice, hit the buds good. She came back with my coins and smiled, like a grandmother at a baptism.

Kramer was on the black. Cue against the chin, lining it up for bottom right. Arrived behind him, said: 'You're shite.'

He took the shot in the same instant, missed the pocket by a small country. 'Well, Charles? Long time.'

Closer inspection showed a shaved head, almost bald. An earring and a pock-marked face. Had more weight up close, muscles turning to flab. He chalked and I took a seat, replied: 'What the fuck is it with this Charles shit? I don't remember bein made no royalty.'

'You're a real prince alright, with the cops at your feet, beggin you to be part of their gang.'

'I didn't invite them. That's compliments of your friend, Joe.'

Simon sunk the black and went about setting up another game. Kramer looked pissed that he'd lost, asked: 'How's the education goin?'

'Finished.'

'What now?'

'I'll think of somethin.'

He rubbed his nose, looked at the Cidona, sniffed and said: 'Still on the dry?'

'Yeah, what's it to ya?'

'Call it concern for your welfare.'

'Ain't you got enough concerns of your own?'

'I got a few, and that's why you're here.'

'Enlighten me.'

'Joe ain't gonna take the fall.'

'Tough cookies.'

'There's shipments gettin intercepted since the day he was nailed. We figure he's talkin like a motherfucker.'

'What's it got to do with me?'

'I wanna wipe him out. The heat is affectin the whole damn business.'

'That doesn't answer my question.'

'I'm gonna use him as an example, a warnin to all the other touts.'

'What about when he goes under with the D.S.? How you gonna find him?'

'That's where you come in.'

He broke. Bad break. The balls were heavy and stubborn. Simon lined up a shot and Kramer took a long draught of cider, said: 'I figure Malone wants you in the programme, which means you'll be gettin close to Joe.'

'So?'

'P.J says you didn't really like him that much.'

'I didn't.'

'Once people know they can't hide behind the law, they'll never talk again.'

I took in some Cidona, asked: 'What the fuck're you talkin about?'

'There's whispers on the street, Charlie. Sayin shit like there's a rat in my crew. People are comin to me, tellin me guys I used to know are talkin to pigs like Malone outside the courthouse. They're sayin that business is sufferin, that somethin needs to be done.'

'Bullshit.'

'When I hear somethin like that, it's my job to take action, to make examples. If I don't, people are gonna start lookin for chinks and takin shots at me. Greedy cunts will try to take over. I got enough fuckin problems.'

'But why me?'

'It has to be you. It's the only way I can be sure you're still solid. It ain't personal.'

I took in some Cidona, said: 'First: if I go in, which I won't, they'll never put us in the same room. Second, if I did take him out, they'll piece it together easy, leavin me as a wide open suspect. And third, I don't owe you anythin, there's nothin in it for me. I don't even know why the fuck I came here.'

Simon intervened. 'You came coz you knew if you didn't, we'd think you had somethin to hide.'

'But I don't know anythin. Even if I was talkin, what would I say? What the fuck do I know?'

'It ain't what you know; it's what people think you know, and it ain't changed much anyway, just got bigger. I don't wanna go down this road with you Charlie, but I'll do what I have to do.'

'But then it's me that gets sent down.'

'It's up to you how you do it. People in Joe's position kill themselves all the time. Once he does, you freak out. Don't want to talk. Stress and all that shit....it happens. It's either this, or you...'

Standoff. Simon took a shot and missed. Kramer drained his pint. Everything smelled of paint. I was trying to figure a way to buy some time. Kramer continued: 'Do this and we end our business here.'

'I went my own way a long time ago.'

'Somethin has to be done.'

'Ain't you worried I'll sell out altogether, give Malone what he wants? It'd be a lot fuckin easier?'

'Word is you already did. I'm giving you a chance to prove them wrong.'

'Fuck you. How many times I gotta prove myself?'

'That's history now.'

'You owe me.'

'I owe no-one.'

'Then neither do I.' Stood to go, took out my smokes and got ready to spark, zipped up my jacket and pulled the collar to my ears.

Kramer picked up the stick and bent to take another shot, said: 'I'll give you a couple of days.'

'I won't need them.'

'Think hard, Charlie. Think hard.' I turned to walk and he stopped me with: 'Oh, and send my regards to your lady.'

Exterior. Lower Salthill. Night. Somewhere in the distance I could hear the walls edge closer, ominous and ruthless. Took a right towards the prom, passed Feeney's shop, Devon Park and Dr. Mannix Road, on towards The Warwick. Figured the coke had gone straight to his head, like he was watching too much *Scarface* or something. Walked on passed Claude's Casino and down by Seapoint. The air was cool, folks stood at the bus stop, looking like they'd been there forever. Took a bench facing the water and collected my thoughts. Had almost a week before I left the country, but knew I'd never live to see it. Got an image of a shadow moving from the darkness, another gangland hit, another statistic. I figured a plan B, long shot, but better odds than sticking around. Went home to run it by El Niño.

Outside, about to turn the key in the door, I heard: 'Move house?'

Malone, standing shoulder to the wall, arms folded. Thought about all sorts of excuses, but knew he had me. 'Just callin in to a friend.'

'With a key?'

'Yeah, what the fuck're you doin here anyway?'

'My job. What were you doing in The Crescent?'

'Playin pool, drinkin Cidona. What's it to you?'

'Kramer was in there too.'

'Oh yeah?'

'You're fuckin around, Charlie. We both know it.'

El Niño heard the talk, opened the door, said: 'Hey.'

Malone walked over, tried sarcasm with: 'Hey.'

She looked him up and down, said: 'Who's this, Charlie?'

'Some weirdo that followed me home.'

He took out the credentials, went: 'Detective Inspector John Malone.'

'And why are you at my house?'

'You live here?'

'Yeah. Now answer my question.'

'I want a word with Charlie. He's a popular man these days.'

'It's ok, go back inside.' She stared at me for a few seconds, then closed the door slowly. I turned with: 'Ok, you finished?'

'She's beautiful.'

'What the fuck do you want?'

'I wanna know what Kramer said to you.'

'It was a chance meetin. We just acknowledged each other.'

'You expect me to believe that?'

'I don't expect anythin, but it's the truth.'

'You had no other reason to be there.'

I shrugged, he said: 'You're not as smart as you think you are.'

'Whatever, but I am cold, so if we can do this another time...?'

He grabbed me by the collar and shoved me against the wall. Gave me two swift knees to the kidneys, pulled me down, knee to the face and threw me on the ground. The keys flew outta my hand. He finished with a couple of kicks into the stomach and one in the teeth, just for the road. All fours was the best recovery I could manage. He bent down. I could smell the cheap aftershave, breath like rotting meat, rancid. He whispered into my ear, spitting all the while. 'The end is coming, Charlie, and it doesn't look pretty.'

I spat blood on the ground and licked a loose tooth with my tongue. I was breathing with heavy, wheezy intakes. He went on. 'You're gonna do what I tell ya. You're gonna send these fuckers down, coz if you don't, it'll be your head, and your pretty girl inside, and all your going straight and college bullshit won't save you. Don't think you fool me with this sober game. You're a fuckin cockroach in my eyes.'

He kicked me in the ribs again, spat and left. I got back inside and El Niño freaked, hand to the mouth, what the hell happened? All that. She went and got bandages, ice cubes wrapped in towels, bottles of disinfectant. I told her the outlines, then explained my plan. She was pissed at first. Then I told her bout the meeting with Kramer and she was convinced.

CHAPTER TWENTY-ONE

Exterior. Eyre Square. Late evening. Dark. Light rain, almost warm. Waiting at the taxi rank. Choked up bus engines and a smell like burnt rubber. I was feeling edgy. Paranoid. Like the bullet was coming, slow and silent. Checked my teeth. They were still sore. Malone the prick. El Niño smoked beside me, suitcase and washed hair. The cab came. We sat in. Scent of leather and cigarettes and cheap aftershave. The driver was from Galway. Had relations in Mayo. Did we know the Mcdonagh's in Castlebar?

Got to Ballinrobe. Paid him and said good luck. Stood in Cornmarket. Air smelled different — less polluted. The town was chilly and quiet, but felt safe. She said: 'This is it?'

'Fraid so.'

'You even have a Supermacs.'

Pointed, said: 'House is just up here.'

We were greeted with a strong draught. The place smelled damp and old. Dank stairs to the right and torn lino on the hall. The wallpaper was falling off in strips and there were cobwebs around the ceiling. Walked through to the sitting room. Same kinda scene with some termite-infested furniture. Dropped the bags, she asked: 'When's the last time someone lived here?'

'Been a long while. Used to be my place before I left for Galway.'

'Years, then. Lovely.'

I lit a smoke. 'We'll sleep here, put down a fire, make it our own.'

'How could you have had a place of your own, when you were so young?'

'After the old man died, it was just me. No one came knockin. I learned to survive.'

She thought about that. Then went. 'So what now?'

'Wait.'

'For what?'

'The plane.'
'Four days?!'
'Aye.'
'Four days here?'
'What else we gonna do?'
'We'll crack up.'
'I don't wanna attract any heat.'
'From Galway?'
'Yeah. They could be connected down here.'
'Hardly?'
'It's a small world.'
'I wanna see the town at least.'
'There ain't much to see.'
'There must be something.'
'You big into tumbleweed?'
She looked around, said: 'This place is a mess.'

She was right. We started cracking up after a few hours. Decided to show her the sights. Figured Kramer would never look for me down here. Or by the time he did, we'd be long gone. The rain was heavy. Wet footpath shone with the glow from the streetlights. We walked through the Christian Brothers schoolyard and into the church grounds. She was intrigued by the chapel windows and wanted to see inside.

Interior. Church. There was a smell of mass just said, like newly burned candles. Benches, light brown. Walked up the aisle, confession box on the right. Altar was round, two steps leading up to it. Mural behind, loud and yellow; depicted the flight from Israel. Chalice left out, tabernacle at the back. Podium with an open bible. She was enthralled and said: 'I love churches.'

Had a butterfly in the gut for no reason. Felt as if I was doing something right and wrong at the same time, like breaking a rule that didn't really exist. El Niño was staring at the windows. She was mesmerised. I walked over, crept almost, kissed her neck lightly. She tasted like coconut. Looked at her focus of interest. Saw depictions of Christ. A myriad of colours. The beginning, the betrayal, the end.

Did the full walk around. She never said a word the whole time. Walked with her, hands in my coat pockets. I longed for her interest, her awe, her wonder. Felt good to draw it out.

Exterior. Outside church. Night. She blessed herself from the fountain of holy water. Made me do the same. Walked towards Main Street. Iron gates and statues on either side. Rain still coming against us, lighter now. Took a right and walked down Main Street. Cars slushed by. Few pedestrians gave us weird looks. Walked passed Inches pub, Martin Murphy's newsagent, and took a right at Golden Fashions.

Got four cans of cider and a bottle of wine in Dermot's off-licence. Place smelled like ale and Ireland. Compact, solid spot. Friendly man behind the counter. Asked if we were local. Told him we were on holidays; down for the weekend. He didn't seem to buy it but said nothing. Got home and put a fire down. Laid a blanket out in front of the flames. She sparked the wine and we got warm, then naked. Later, when she was merry, she lifted her glass and said: 'Here's to being on the run.'

'We'll save the Champagne for London.'

'This town isn't so bad. Quiet, but serene.'

I lit a smoke, said: 'You liked the church?'

'Yeah, the windows. They're beautiful.'

'Ain't been there since I was a kid.'

She took the cigarette from me, said: 'Philistine.'

'That mean I got no religion? I'm dealin with a nun here?'

'No, it means you don't appreciate art.'

'What's there to appreciate?'

'Immortality.'

'Here we go.'

'The guy that crafted the windows, his name was Clarke.'

'Yeah?'

'Yeah, and the only reason I know that is because he was recognised for his work. He was an artistic genius.'

'So?'

She left down the cigarette, sat up and rolled her eyes, pushed her hair behind her ears. Her face was warm from the heat of the fire. 'Look, the guy's dead, yeah? And we're still talking about him, so that means his memory lives on. He's become immortal through his art.'

'But I still never heard of him.'

'Until now.'

'Ain't changed me much.'

'Yeah, but at least he's not forgotten.'

Instrumental. 'Let me guess, you wanna be immortal?'

'I dunno.'

'Could be like your old man said — there's a way you're meant to live.'

'I don't wanna disappoint him.'

'I think you're doin ok.'

'I fuckin hope so. I just don't wanna go down at the hands of a couple of cokeheads. I got a helluva lot more to do.'

'Don't worry about it. We're nearly in the clear.'

'You think they know we're down here?'

'They'll be gettin suss from tomorrow on, but they'll exhaust Galway first. We just gotta lie low.'

She lay back against my feet, said: 'I never told you about my friend Caroline.'

'Why would ya?'

'When I think of us on the run, it reminds me of her.'

'Where's she now?'

'It's a long story.'

'We have all night.'

'Yeah, but I just get scared when I think about it.'

'A tough chick like you?'

'I'm serious. It scares me because of the situation we're in.'

'Somethin to do with Kramer?'

'I don't know. I don't think so.'

'Drugs then?'

'Yeah.'

'Ok, just tell me.'

She took another drink, assembled the story in her head, and began.

CHAPTER TWENTY-TWO

'We met in first year. She was just like me, all about living it up, and almost as beautiful. It wasn't long into the first term and we started fooling around with these two guys. They weren't in college but they were always hanging about. One of them had a really nice car and they'd pick us up after lectures. They had an apartment in Renmore and we'd go there and get high and do all sorts of crazy shit. It was fun, experimental, but fun.

'Don't think I want the details.'

''Bout six weeks into it, Caroline starts really liking the drugs. It wasn't just fun for her any more. She wanted them all the time and was pissed when she couldn't get any. We never asked where they got their gear. They didn't have jobs or anything, but they were full of cash. We weren't fuckin stupid, we knew they were dealing — but that just added to the excitement. That was us, call it illegal and we came knocking.'

'Coke?'

'Yeah. Acid; smoke, bit of coke, everything, but I drew the line with needles. Caroline didn't. She started staying at their house and missing a lot of college. In the end, we were starting to drift. When I'd go out there, it wasn't like we'd all be getting high together, it was the three of them there all day, snorting and shooting up and fuckin each other stupid. When I'd come in they were all either too doped out to know I was there, or so fuckin high that it wasn't worth my while even trying to catch up — and forget about the relationships.'

'How do you mean?'

'I went out there one day and found Caroline taking it from my guy in the mouth and her man was having her from behind while the whole thing was being fed into a camcorder. After that, I just walked. I didn't want to be a part of it any more. I went home and puked, I was really fuckin sickened at myself, and rattled. What if I'd gotten that wasted? Caroline didn't even know what the fuck was going on. As long as they kept feeding her gear, she'd keep sucking them clean and taking it from all available angles.'

'They never wondered why you left?'

'I got a few calls, mostly late at night. It was usually her, and sometimes the guy I'd been seeing. I never answered but they left voicemails, asking me to call over, saying they missed me around and I'm losing out on a whole lotta fun. She came across as wasted all the time, but he always sounded slimy, like he was luring me. I never answered; I just got on with my life. There's times when I feel pretty guilty for not doing more to save her.'

'That's the last time you saw her?'

'No. About two months after the porn show, I called out there. I was all fit to run in, slap her awake and throw her into a waiting taxi. Enough was enough. I coulda called the cops but; I didn't know who the fuck I was dealing with. What if they thought I was some kind of tout?

So I call a cab. It's after Christmas and it's a cold motherfuckin night. My heart's beating and all I wanna do is tell the driver to turn round and bring me home. I'm cursing the day I met these guys and even deep down there's a voice saying I shoulda cut Caroline loose a long time ago. But I can't think like that. She was a friend, and I liked her, and I had a duty to come through, fuck it.

We pull up at the house and there's lights inside. I can hear music and I know there's more than three people in there. I tell the cabbie to wait and he says he can't do more than five minutes coz he's got other calls.

I knock and a man answers, looks me up and down, asks: 'What you want?' I've never seen him before but he's rougher than the other two. Smells like sweat and cigarettes. I tell him I'm here to talk to Caroline and he says she's busy. I tell him it won't take long, but he says she's not available. Then he takes a good look at my chest and starts to think a bit and asks if I'm looking for gear. I figure this can get me in, so I tell him I want a hit. He smiles and pulls the door back and asks why the hell I didn't just say so.

We get inside and the place is a mess. There's beer cans, stale food, dirty needles, the whole fuckin works thrown around the place. The music's banging out some Chemical Brothers and a couple of wasted guys are on the couch, belts on their arm, in another fuckin world. From the kitchen I can hear shouts and cheers. I ask the guy that let me in what's going on and he laughs and leads me through.

There, a crowd of guys are all on their knees and they've formed a circle around something on the floor and they're all masturbating. There's a lotta shouting and abuse, but I still can't see what's in the middle. I walk up and realise it's a body, the body of a woman and she's naked. In the same instant, I realise it's Caroline. She's out cold and looking a bit blue and for a second I thought she was dead. I turn to the doorman and ask him what the hell they're doing and he tells me it's a competition - the last one to cum gets to fuck her properly.'

'Jesus.'

'Yeah. I wanna go in there and pull her out, kick them all away and drag her into the taxi, but I know it's pointless. If I start kicking up, making a fuss, who the hell knows what they're gonna do to me?

Then the dealer takes me gently by the elbow, turns me around and says: 'So what exactly will you be looking for?' He winks and continues with: 'And more importantly, how will you be paying?

At this stage the shouting's getting louder, reaching a crescendo and I don't wanna think about why. This guys got no teeth, but he's smiling like it's still Christmas and the junkies on the couch are tryna use their legs. One makes a good effort but trips over the table, stumbles and cracks his head off the fireplace. This distracts the dealer and I make a run for it. Outside, the cabbie's just pulling away but I shout and he hears me. And I get home all shook up but still determined to help her somehow, ya know?

I make a trek out there again around 3 the following afternoon. All morning I have that image in my head of those guys sitting around, and while it puts me off, it makes me angry too. So I figure I'll get a cab in Eyre Square and hope the fuckers are all too doped to know I'm there...they usually are at that time of the day anyway...

I come around by Eglington Street and I'm walking up toward the rank when she calls me. I hear this 'Niño!' and I look around and there she is. Dressed like shit and looking like she's just been exhumed. I ask what the fuck is going on and tell her about the night before. She tries to act horrified; says it wasn't her. Then she backtracks a bit and says she was a bit wasted; but it was probably all in the name of good fun. I tell her she's gone too far and she needs help but she doesn't want to hear it. All the time I think she's building up to something. Then she asks if I'm looking for any gear. Turns out, she's started dealing to feed her own habit. I tell her to forget it. She gets a bit pissed then, asks me who the fuck I think I am, and what makes me better than her, all that. I take it for a while, but in the end I just walk and resign myself to the fact that I tried.'

'You haven't seen her since?'

'Couple of months later, down by the docks, I saw her on the game. She spotted me coming, but there was no acknowledgement on either side. I just kept on walking.'

'Fuck...'

'Yeah, but here's the freaky thing. One day that summer, it's just after the exams and I'm at home, waiting for this guy to call and take me out. It's about 9 o'clock and he's due at 9.30. I'm ready early, so I switch on the TV to pass the time. News comes on. Headlines are pretty typical except for one about a murder in Dublin, a young girl. Figured she musta been shot or something but then it goes into the details. Turns out she was from Galway. The news says she was making a delivery for an organised crime gang and was the victim of a feud. They found a stash of dodgy snow beside her. The Galway crew had used her as a mule to try and offload it to the Dublin crews — if it went wrong, she was expendable. Once the Dubs found out the coke was bad, they killed her. After that, it shows a picture and it's Caroline. I get a bit freaked out, knowing that I knew her once, but there's relief there too.'

'Relief?'

'Yeah. Selfish relief because I got out of the whole thing before it went that far, and relief for her because she was free from all the shit. She'd have never escaped any other way.'

'And they just shot her?'

'Standard rape. Mutilation, cigarette burns, cattle prods, that type of thing — and then the signature.'

'Crucifixion?'

'Cut her fuckin throat with a shears.'

Later, when she was asleep, the fire illuminated the room and my hand danced in a shadow across the ceiling. I was real wound up. Listening for the door, adrenaline going. Instincts always ready for an attack. Thought about the decision to run. For the best. Wanted out. There was no other way. One side or the other wanted to hang me.

I turned towards El Niño. Her face in the night. She smelled like cider. It seeped into my pores like temptation. Knew it was a bad time to slip. All the arguments came up. Like a one-off session and the ease of stopping. Like the docs were wrong, or exaggerating. Like there was a way I could blank out for a few days and recover fine.

Kept it at bay and thought more. I knew there was never any coming back. Ireland was over. No identity here, a criminal history and an Arts degree. I was technically clear, but cunts like Malone would never let it slide. It was like a black spot on my soul.

Stayed alert til about six and then my lids got heavy. Dawn brought a small peace, end of the night and demons. Flames were dying as I pulled over the covers.

I dreamt of crazy things. The past, my father, El Niño being tortured. Falling off the wagon.

CHAPTER TWENTY-THREE

The next day. We walked into The Cider Tiger at about 3 o'clock. I knew I'd've never let myself leave town without a look. Everything flooded back, helped by the fact that the place hadn't changed. Even Jane was still behind the counter, looking older now, better, but slightly bitter. Day drinkers at the bar, checking her out. Asking questions like: 'What time are ya finished?'

She watched the door as we entered. Place was divided in two, like a double dining room. Went through to the back. Saw the ghost of myself everywhere. Twiddled a beer mat, no change in infrastructure. Pool table on the right. Dartboard on the left. Someone had stuck three darts into the bullseye. A name was scribbled in chalk on the black surface beside it. Bar was bright wooden. Budweiser, Carlsberg, Guinness and Heineken, all giving me the wink. Passage ahead that led to the front. Heard Jane's footsteps coming through. Thought of all the times she had served me the poison. That, and the shit I'd given her. She appeared, still hadn't recognised me, said: 'Hi, what can I get ye?'

Let the realisation kick in. She looked, observed and clicked. 'Oh my god, Charlie?'

'That's me, sugar.'

'Jesus, wow, how long…? How come you're home?'

'Just a flyin visit, Jane. Couldn't pass without a look at the place.'

She looked at El Niño. Then took a glass in her hand. 'I heard…lotsa things. About you, Galway and Kramer, what…? Let me get you a drink…'

'Yeah sure. Can of cider for the lady, Cidona for me. Pint glass and ice.'

She frowned, bewildered for a second, then set about it. Came back and left them down. I tried to pay but she said: 'That's on me.' Then asked: 'So, what've you been up to?'

'Bits and pieces. This and that.'

'Always the dark horse. Someone said you went and got educated.'

'Yeah, give it a name.'

'Fair play, and what're y'at now?'

'Entrepreneur in the business of life.'

She laughed and hit me with a towel. I introduced her to El Niño. They were cordial. We made some more small talk, then she said: 'I'll be out the front if you want me. Paul should be home from work in a while.'

I turned to the pool table, asked El Niño: 'How're ya fixed for a game?'

'Let's do it.'

I racked 'em up and she went to the jukebox. Put on The Pixies. Game went to the black and I hung it on purpose. Felt like a gentleman. She said: 'I don't want your fuckin sympathy.'

We racked another and I wasted her. Then she came back on frame three and wiped me out. I called Jane and ordered another round. She asked: 'Am I right in saying you're on the dry?'

'That'd be correct.'

She seemed relieved, said: 'Oh Charlie, that's great.'

'That's cool, Jane. It's been a while now, but thanks.'

I paid her this time, told her to take one for herself. She did, gave me the change and said: 'Thanks, Charlie.'

The back door opened and I heard: 'Well now, here's a blast from the past.'

For a frightening second I thought it was my father, then I turned and said: 'Howya doin, Paul?'

He was home from a day of plastering. Covered in random splashes of cement. Still had the tache, but the years were starting to show. It was subtle, just a small bend in the back and a few wrinkles under the eyes. We shook hands with real affection. I introduced him to El Niño. He was all friendly and apologised for the state of his clothes. Jane came out and he shouted a round. Was impressed when I asked for Cidona. We sat back, sipped and got ready for some catching up. He wanted to know everything. Where I'd been, what had happened in Galway, plans for the future. Told him the outlines, that we were finished college and wanted to do some travelling. Raised his eyebrows when I talked about the degree. Left out the criminal aspects, but I could tell he was reading between the lines. He tried to trace El Niño's roots, asking bout her parents, wondering if he knew them, but he gave up after a while. The silence hit and he got to the point. 'So when did ya give up the sauce?

'Few years done now.'

'You're doin well so.'

'Alright. No slips yet.'

'God willin there won't be.'

'Business good here?'

'Middlin. Want out of it now. Sick of the same craic all the time. Town is riddled with drugs. I haven't much time for the young crowd anymore.'

Instrumental. He broke it with: 'Where's Kramer now?'

'Still in the big smoke.'

'Did he cop himself on?'

'No. Haven't seen him much in the last few years.'

'Some prick that fella.'

The door swung open. We all looked. One of the hardcore punters from the early days of robbing. Black leather jacket, knuckledusters, and lotsa face metal. Jane came in from the front bar, wasn't happy to see him, said: 'Yeah?'

He handed out €50 said: 'Gimme change'

'Not without a purchase.'

'I want to buy fags.'

She sighed and took the note. Paul stared like a bull itching to charge. She checked it for counterfeit. Gave him the coins and went back out to the front. Cigarette machine was beside us. He came over, put the money in and got the smokes. Looked our way. Gave the nod and left.

Paul said: 'Fellas like him would want to be buried to the head and stoned.'

'Used to know him years back.'

'He's an awful waste of space.'

Jane came back, shaking her head, said: 'I hate that fucker.'

El Niño said: 'Looks like he needs a visit from the fashion police.'

'He's a druggy bastard.'

'A user?'

'A fuckin dealer. His name's Anthony, or Anto. Always trying to push the stuff on to young lads. Bet he was just in now seeing who's around.'

'He in to anythin big?'

'Think it's mostly smoke, but then someone said he's started on...'

She was called by a customer and had to run to the front. I had to go to the Jacks anyway.

Interior. Bathroom. Two urinals and a cubicle. Mirror on the left. Did my thing and Paul came in. We were awkward for a second, then he said: 'She's a helluva woman, Charlie.'

'Who're ya tellin?'

'You'd want to take care of her.'

I zipped up, washed my hands. He said: 'Everythin else alright?'

'How'd ya mean?'

'You know — you on the straight and narrow?'

'Yeah, cheers Paul. It's all good.'

'Anythin I can do for ya?'

'Like what?'

'You alright for cash?'

'Yeah, we're ok.'

I brushed my wet hands through my hair and he asked: 'You sure?'

'Yeah, sure I'm sure. What's with the concern?'

'Nothin, but I'm not stupid. I know when there's more to a story. If you're in a bit of shit, just tell me. I'll help in any way I can.'

'There's nothin to worry about, I'm doin fine. Thanks, Paul.'

'You were a good lad, Charlie. I was sorry we left things the way we did.'

'That's all history now.'

'Thanks be ta God.'

And he walked out.

Back at the bar. The women were talking about the art of travel. We took our seats, chatted some more and wrapped things up after an hour. I hugged Jane goodbye, and Paul walked us to the door. He gave El Niño an awkward embrace and me another handshake, said: 'Remember what I told ya. Anythin I can do.'

Exterior. Evening. The Cider Tiger car park. The day's light in the dying stages. Vehicle ahead, black. Honda Civic. Windows tinted, movement behind them. Lights flashed twice. I knew it meant an invitation to come over. El Niño had her hand crooked in my arm. Warning signals were screaming, not that I ever paid them much attention. We got to the wheels. Electric glass came down, gave us a face.

'Alright, Charlie man, how's the craic?'

Hand came out, I took it. It was warm, rough, said: 'Anto, been a while.'

'Sure has. Wanna go for a spin?'

'Not today, man. Lot to do. Some other time?'

He gave El Niño the once over, longer than was social. Then: 'What you been doin with yourself? Heard all sortsa crazy shit like you conformed.'

'All lies, Anto. Had to keep the heat off my back.'

'I hear ya. It was good what you did that time — takin the fall and all.'

I made no comment. He lit a smoke, said: 'How's the trade up there?'

'Good. Lotta dough on show.'

'And the man with the plan?'

'Top form.'

'Helps us all. Things just takin off here, but there's potential, ya know?'

He looked right at me. The whites of his eyes were a light shade of yellow. Smoke floated around the upholstery. I said: 'I guess that's all ya need.'

Silence. Figured the exchange was over. Stood straight to leave. He turned the key a notch, said: 'Tell him you were talkin to me.'

The engine roared to life and he pulled away. Wheelspins. Gravel flying, exhaust roaring. Exit Anto. El Niño said: 'Fuck.'

'I know. It just gets better and better.'

'What now?'

'Stick to the plan.'

'But he's gonna tell Kramer.'

'I don't think he knows the story.'

'Fuck, Charlie.'

'It's ok.'

'It's not, we're fucked. We have to get outta here.'

'Relax.'

'We can't relax. We're not safe anymore.'

'Babe, listen. You're trustin me, remember? I got it under control.'

'Yeah but they'll know we left the city now.'

'Don't panic.'

'We could just leave. Get outta the country now, forget the money. We'll make some more.'

'Forget fifty grand?'

'Yeah, if it beats getting chopped up.'

'Look, it's fine. Two days and we're gone. It ain't that long to wait.'

'I'm shaking. I can handle the pigs, and the bullshit, but the rest of it just freaks me out. You know it does.'

'You're talkin crazy. Listen to yourself. We have a plan and it's gonna work.'

'Fuck it, Charlie, let's run now. Let's pack our shit and go. I don't want the money. This is not why my folks left it to me. They didn't want me to *die* over it.'

'We're gonna be ok. We're just waitin, that's all.'

She wasn't convinced. I said: 'I think he's just small-time. He's probably not connected at all. Just tryna sound hard.'

'What if you're wrong?'

'It doesn't matter. What matters is us — us gettin away. If we're gonna do it we have to stay calm, alright?'

'Fuck.'

'Calm.'

I pulled her close, said: 'I won't let them hurt ya.'

She dug her head in to my chest, went: 'What if they get to you first?'

CHAPTER TWENTY-FOUR

They kicked in the door the next morning. Heard the hinges coming. It wasn't the big crash you'd see on the screen; it took a few attempts. We got dressed in between, ready for the confrontation. I knew straight away it wasn't Kramer. Only cops would make that amount of noise. Heard shoulders and feet thumping off the wood, then something hard, like a gas barrel, breaking through. Expected them to do the procedure, back against the wall, gun poised 007 style, taking no chances.

Instead, they came with stupid looks, checking out the place. Two monkeys, Tango and Cash, Irish style. Tango went upstairs, flashing a torch. Cash came in, bright yellow jacket, armed with a baton. Expected him to say: 'You have the right to remain silent' or 'Ain't this a pretty sight?'

Instead, he said: 'Get up, ya little druggy bollocks.'

He stared at El Niño. I said: 'Get the fuck outta my house.'

'Not gonna work this time, boyo.'

'What're ya talkin about?'

'Call from up above. There's a certain Detective Inspector who's eager to talk to you.'

'Who's that then?'

'The name *Malone* ring a bell?'

Tango came down, belly and blue eyes, gave El Niño a double-take, said: 'Clear upstairs.'

He pointed at me. 'He's all we need anyway.'

'What about the girl?'

'Fuck her. We only want him for now.'

I went for Tango. He was fitter than he looked, took me down in a chokehold. El Niño was in fast and gave him an empty bottle of wine over the head. Glass smashed and scattered, danced on the ground. Tango collapsed all blood and shock. Cash shook his chins and took out a baton and hit me on the arm. Christ, it hurt. She ran in, shouting: 'Get the fuck off him!'

He went. 'Shut up ya little bitch!' And gave her a slap.

It was loud, came with a crack. A trickle of blood came down the side of her mouth. I took exception to that. Gave him my best right hook to the jaw, put him off balance and the baton fell. I picked it up. Tango was on his feet again. Knocked him clean out with one swing. Got working on Cash. Hard violent attacks. Bones breaking, him roaring for mercy. Gave me insane satisfaction. She was breathing beside me, hand on my shoulder, said: 'Bastards.'

There was a bruise on her cheek and her bottom lip was starting to swell. I was getting calm now, collected. Took her hand, asked: 'You ok?'

She nodded, swallowed and said: 'We should get the fuck outta here.'

We collected some things. Went for it. Got to the front door. Sensations on autopilot. Camera shaky. Had plans to steal a motor and work it from there. Twenty-four hours to the flight. She was coming behind me. Frantic thoughts.

Exterior. Street. Saw sunlight and people walking dogs. And passing cars. A kid screamed somewhere in the distance. Then a movement behind me, with a flash like the sun had exploded. Thought I was having an aneurysm. Just before I fell, I heard Malone, incredulous, asking: 'Where the fuck do you think *you're* going?'

El Niño screamed as my grip slipped. I tried to shout but I was unconscious before I hit the ground.

-

All cells are the same: white, ugly, stink. Bad beds. Woke up and thought I'd been drinking. Then the movie played. The scene, the cops, the reality. Was on my own, felt like I was being quarantined. Figured they'd put El Niño in a separate cage. Had slept in my clothes. Head pounded like the supernova of migraines. Arm in serious pain. Smell of soup and ink. Fan overhead that didn't work. Window behind me, getting dark outside. Door opened. Tango came in. He was limp. Plaster on the elbow, swollen jaw, looking bitter. He mumbled: 'You're wanted above.'

'Any chance of a Panadol?'

'Up, ya prick. You'll be lucky if I don't give you a shoe in the hole.'

'That's hospitality.'

'Don't get fuckin smart.'

Sat on the edge of the bed, rubbed my eyes. He was irritated. Started twirling keys in his good hand. Sweat coming through, mixed with a vest. He smelled like a turf box. Headache screamed. I looked up, went: 'You wouldn't have a spare?'

He wheezed hard, took out the baton, said: 'If you don't get off that fuckin bed...'

He led me to a room that said: PRIVATE. Malone was inside. Smoking, looking sombre, like an audition for *The Streets of San Francisco*. Sat down and Tango left us alone. The door fell closed with an echo. There was silence. He pushed the smokes my way. I sparked. He was looking me over. The light flickered overhead. I felt sort of uncomfortable, like I'd just gotten his daughter pregnant.

'Week's up, Charlie.'

'It would appear so.'

'What the fuck're ya doing down here?'

My arm ached some more. 'Takin a break.'

'Hiding out.'

'Give it a name.'

'Your back's to the wall. You know it, I know it. Time to come across.'

'It's never time with me, John. That's what your people will never understand about ours.'

He sighed, said: 'That's a shame.'

'Sure is.'

'You should consider your situation before you make any concrete decisions.'

'I made a concrete decision a week ago.'

'Circumstances have changed.'

'But not my principles.'

'Your principles are based on convenience. You've never had anything truly personal to lose.'

'I presume this is goin somewhere.'

He tipped some ash, said: 'Every man has a weakness, Charlie, an...*Achilles* heel.'

Figured there was no reply. Said nothing. He stood up, paced back and over. I dragged hard, waiting for the revelation. Then it hit me. 'Where is she?'

'We let her go.'

'That's not what I asked.'

'We don't know where she is.'

'But you know she's not safe. Why're you such a fuckin scumbag?'

'We only had reason to arrest you.'

'That's hardly the point.'

He shrugged and sat back down. We did the staring thing. I read his thoughts, said: 'You're usin her as bait.'

'They're looking for you, Charlie. And sooner or later, they're gonna come down here.'

'She's not a pawn in your sick game.'

'I do what I have to do.'

'We both know she's innocent.'

'They'll use anything to protect themselves, including blackmail.'

'Suppose they're not that different from you fucks so.'

He let it slide. I said: 'You think I won't talk now? You should see me if anythin happens to her.'

'We won't be the ones to hurt her.'

'But you'll put her life in danger to get what you want.'

'That's unfortunate, but yes. This is a war, Charlie, and there will be casualties.'

'It was never my war.'

'You got involved of your own accord.'

'Not in the snow.'

'Crime is crime.'

'Then leave her out of it.'

'I can't prevent that. Only you can.'

'Bullshit.'

'We'll put her on the programme too. But first you have to agree to testify.'

'Not before I find her.'

He looked around the room, stubbed his smoke, looked back and said: 'You've met Anto?'

I shrugged, said: 'Who the fuck is Anto?'

He took out a dictaphone, pressed play, began in mid-conversation. Unmistakeable voices.

Kramer:	'You're sure it's him?'
Anto:	'Yeah, we even talked for a while.'
Kramer:	'Fucker's hidin out, gettin ready to roll over for Malone.'
Anto:	'That's what I reckon.'
Kramer:	'Keep an eye on him. Him and his fuckin doll.'
Anto:	'Want me to make an example of him down *here*?'
Kramer:	(*pause*) Do whatever the fuck you need to do, just get him outta the way.
Anto:	Roger that.

Beat.

Kramer:	How much you want this time?
Anto:	Double the last.
Kramer:	Cash on delivery?
Anto:	Yeah.
Kramer:	I'll see ya down there.

Click.

Malone pressed pause with deliberation, lips pursed. I tried a poker face. He said: 'We followed a shipment down here a month ago. We tapped Anto when we saw him make the pick-up. He's been in regular contact with Kramer for months. When we build enough evidence, we're gonna take him down.'

'Still none of my business.'

'I need you to seal it. With this and what we have from Joe, Kramer'll get ten years and be out in five. With you talking, we can indict him from the beginning, all the way back to Max. He'll get life if he's lucky.'

'What if I say no?'

'Then I arrest you right now for the job on Chartbusters, and your girlfriend stays in danger. He's coming down here tonight with a huge instalment; it's the perfect coup. Anto was watching when we arrested you...'

'I'll never say a word until I know she's safe.'

'But you will talk?'

'I'll do nothin without her.'

He jumped off the seat, said: 'Then go get her.'

'What?'

'Go get her. We don't know where's she's gone.'

'Well how the fuck am I supposed to know?'

'It's your town, and it's not exactly a metropolis. It can't be that hard.'

'What then?'

'Come back here. We'll talk about your future as a new man. New life, new identity.'

'And her?'

'Same.'

'You really think I'm gonna sell out?'

'I don't think you have a choice, and, judging by the tape, I don't think you owe anything to anyone now.'

He turned to the wall. As if the conversation was over. I stood up fast. The chair fell behind me with a plastic thud.

Stole the dictaphone and left.

Exterior. Outside the police station. Late evening. Came down the dip at the end of High Street. Walked fast. Cars driving by, slow and going nowhere. I was hoping that she was hiding out at the house, waiting for me to get back.

Interior. Smelled the violence immediately. The place was wrecked. Shit smashed on the ground, windows broken all around. The crunch from walking on glass. Sitting room: couch overturned, table broken, clothes scattered on the floor. Went upstairs, same story, everything fuckin wrecked. No sign of her anywhere.

My phone rang. It was P.J. I knew what had happened. Even since I'd left the station. Now I had to face it. 'Heya, Charlie.'

'Where the fuck is she?'

'She's safe.'

'Where?'

'We're at the old barracks.'

'The fuck're you doin down there?'

'Waitin for you to come find us.'

'I'm on my way.'

'Better hurry, she's real purty and...'

I hung up. The sky was cloudless and cold. The barracks was just behind the rugby pitch. Went down the steep Bowers Hill and over the bridge. The quiet rhythms of my feet like heartbeats. Heard the voices as I got close. Shouting, bottles smashing, all that. Saw the red tips of their smokes. Reminded me of the first meeting with Kramer's crew.

At the barracks. There was a smell of grass and cowshit and cider. P.J. was counting money in the corner, Simon watched. There was a large suitcase of Cocaine on the ground. Anto and Kramer were arguing over the quantity. The place had no roof and strong stone walls. The chill night poured in from outside. I looked for El Niño straight away. Couldn't see her anywhere.

They saw me and got to attention. Anto said: 'Bout time.'

P.J. stood up, stopped counting, gave me a long look. Simon took out his gun. Kramer was drinking a bottle of Buckfast. He swigged, threw it aside and went: 'You've made up your mind, then?'

'I want my girl.'

'That's why you're hangin out in cop stations?'

'I had no choice. Malone's here too.'

'We know.'

He lit a smoke. I said: 'You want the truth, he ain't here for me.'

'Just for the scenery then?'

'No, because of Anto — I'm just a bonus.'

Anto said: 'The fuck're you talkin about?'

Kramer, laughing: 'What you tryna pull, Charlie?'

'I just want out. This is not my mess.'

He dragged, said: 'It's too late for that.'

'Where is she?'

Gave another scan around. There was a dark room to the right hand corner. Maybe there. P.J was watching everything, me especially. Still had his boxer shirt, wearing a cap too. Kramer was in a leather jacket. Black shirt inside, stomach protruding, gold watch. He walked towards me. Trying to be aggressive. Looking fat.

His breath smelled like garlic and his teeth were crooked and yellow. Up close, he had acne, mouth ulcers, craters in his face and drawn, bloodshot eyes. An acrid smell. He smiled, said: 'Party's over, Charlie.'

'Maybe, but not just for me.'

'Yeah, your girl too.'

'Malone's had you twigged ever since you been shippin down here.'

He looked for the lie in my eyes. I was deadpan. He said: 'Bullshit.'

'He doesn't even need me no more. Heard the tapes myself.'

'You're gettin desperate. I expected more from someone like you.'

'Anto's been tapped. You brought a shipment down here tonight — double last month's. Cash on delivery. How would I know somethin like that...?' He looked back at Anto. I kept going. 'You're startin to break into the small towns. You called Anto, he said I was down here, you told him to stake me out, me and *my fuckin doll*...'

He was breathing heavy, thought he was gonna attack, said: 'You're full of shit.'

I went to pull out the dictaphone.

'Keep your fuckin hands where I can see 'em.'

'I'm takin out proof. You tell me your shipments are gettin busted, accusin me of talkin to the cops, sellin the fuck out, and all the time it's dickheads like Joe and Anto that're causin all your problems....'

'You can't show me fuck all.'

P.J approached, looked at Kramer, asked: 'The fuck is he talkin about?'

The other two came and stood either side. Simon went: 'Just fuckin kill him, Kramer. You know he's gatherin stats for Malone. We gotta get back anyway.'

'Yeah,' said Anto. 'Fuck him.'

'Anto,' Said Kramer. 'Charlie thinks you been tapped, that the fuzz been watchin your moves. What you gotta say bout that?'

'Bollocks.'

'That's what I say, but now he tells me he can prove it and I'm curious. You know what we do with a piece of shit like that?'

He sounded less confident, said: 'Yeah, you cut out his heart and stuff it down his fuckin throat. He gets wiped the fuck out...just like we're gonna do to Charlie here...'

'You hear that, Charlie?'

'You let me take this damn thing out, you'll have all the evidence you need. Then me and my girl walk the fuck outta here, agreed?'

'Cover him, Simon.'

I took out the dictaphone with a calm hand. Simon had the gun pointed to the side of my head. 'I stole this from Malone's office an hour ago.'

Pressed play. Everyone listened. There was confusion at first, then Anto went pale. P.J caught him and twisted his arms behind his back. Simon swung the gun in his direction and we all watched Kramer for a response. He was swift and immediately violent. Gave him two rapid head butts and then they knocked him to the ground. Anto screamed, like he'd been set on fire: 'It's all fuckin lies!'

I took advantage of the distraction to look for El Niño. Found a doorway to the other room. It was dark and dank and smelled like piss. Big stones on the ground and weeds and old cans of battered empty lager. I walked in and scraped my hand off a rusty nail. It drew blood but my adrenaline was too spiked to care. I was fearing the worst, like the moments before you enter a funeral. Moved in further, like going into a cave. Nearly tripped over an empty beer bottle. Heard someone moaning. Looked down. She was on the ground, all tied up, trying to break free. At first I was relieved, then the rage took over. There was no doubt about it. I was going to kill someone. They'd put an old shirt around her mouth to stop her screaming. I tore it away. She went. 'Charlie?'

Her clothes were torn and her cheeks were bruised. I pushed back her hair and there were scratchmarks on her neck. Once her hands were free, she hugged me and started crying, gripping me tight with small, tearful vibrations. 'They did things to me, Charlie. Get me the fuck outta here.'

'It's ok. We're goin. It's over.'

'Jesus Christ. Oh, Jesus Christ.'

'I have ya now.'

'They...'

'Don't think about it...we're goin, we're leavin...it's over'

'Let's go, then....please...just fuckin bring me away...'

I moved back to the door, listened for a few seconds Anto had stopped screaming. Then I heard Kramer say: 'Time to kill this motherfucker.'

Picked up a heavy rock. She said: 'What're you doing?'

'Just wait here a second, don't move.'

'Charlie?'

'One second. Then we're gone. I promise.'

Walked out. Kramer had a gun in his hand, pointed at Anto. He pulled the trigger. Loud shot. Big echo. Tough shit for Anto. One less cunt in the world. I took a swing at P.J from behind and caught him under the ear. It made a crunching sound, like breaking eggshells. It felt good, the tiger inside me loose, roaring for genocide. Simon turned in surprise, looked at the rock, then at P.J. I caught him across the jaw and followed through with another to the top of the skull. Fairly sure his head split open. Kramer swung round, pointed the gun right at me. Moment of truth. There was a second pause, like in the movies, then we heard: 'Hold it right there!'

We both looked back as they spilled towards us. A stampede of police, lights, guns, noise — fuckers even had Uzis.. Kramer fired a shot in their direction. Managed to hit one of them. He fell with a groan and the others opened fire. Suddenly it's a warzone. Bullets flying, people shouting. I ran back and covered El Niño. She was screaming. Hands over her ears. Crazy noise from the guns. And splinters of stone chipping of the walls when they got hit. Rode it out. Kept her close, made sure she was covered from stray bullets. It was like waiting for a violent tornado to pass. I looked up and saw Kramer escape through a back window. They kept firing for a few seconds. Then things went quiet. My ears were ringing. My chest tight, legs shaking, like I'd survived a car accident and the shock was setting in. Her lips were quivering. She looked me right in the eye. In a way that said: Is anything worth this? *Are you?*

Silence.

Their flashlights danced on the ground.

I brought down her hands. They were still covering her ears. 'It's ok. They stopped shootin.'

She sniffled and wiped the tears from her face. I didn't wanna think about what they'd done. I took off my jacket and wrapped it round her shoulders. Could sense the cops drawing closer.

'We need you to walk out SLOWLY with your HANDS behind your HEAD!'

She was shivering and breathing heavy. I whispered: 'We're gonna stand up and be calm, ok?' She nodded. 'There's nothin to worry bout, trust me.'

'I'm so scared, Charlie.'

'It's ok.'

'YOU HAVE TWENTY SECONDS TO WALK OUT OF THERE!'

'Are you ready?'

She choked back some tears, shuddered a bit. 'Ok.'

We walked out. They came round us. Helmets. Bulletproof jackets and radio static and trigger-happy. We slowly raised our hands. I felt exposed, vulnerable, a little afraid. One of them moved in and frisked me. He was young, angry, aggressive, tempting me to make a move against him. Give him a reason to fuck me up. The others stood by and ready. Kramer had shot one of their own and you could tell they wanted justice. There was talk on their radios about an ambulance. Looking for directions. Condition of the wounded officer.

One of the others shouted. 'SIR, does he have a WEAPON, please confirm.'

There were sirens in the distance. A smell of smoke and something like sulphur. Blood warm and racing. I was wondering where the fuck Malone was. How they found us. All that. He moved on to El Niño. Hurt her at times. Not too sure how it was going to play from here. My mouth was dry. A light wind blew. I got the scent of El Niño's hair, her body. It felt good, like we were going to be ok. They'd do Kramer for murder and maybe there was a way out for us.

Then. 'SIR! Is everything OK, sir?!'

He kept frisking her. She got uncomfortable. Started to back away. He told her to stop fuckin around. She looked at me and I said: 'Hey, maybe take it easy...'

'You take it fuckin easy!'

'It's not us you're after!'

'How the fuck do you know who I'm after?!'

'You already checked her and found nothin.'

The others were getting more edgy. Moving in a little closer. Waiting for the word to shoot.

He pushed me against the wall with: 'Why don't you calm the fuck down?'

I pushed him back with. 'You calm the fuck down!'

'SERGEANT, AWAITING COMMAND, SIR!'

He came at me again. I hit him. He fell back. There was a commotion. Some shouting. Then somebody fired.

The shot was loud, close range, cracked the air and came out the other side of her stomach. All that slow motion shit is true.

You see someone take a bullet, it stays with you for the rest of your life. Your memory goes into overdrive and captures every second.

Her eyes got wide, full of surprise. I could see the crisis in her brain. She put a hand to the wound and fell back against the cold stone wall.

The shooter was shocked and looked at the gun as if he'd never seen it before. The rest of them just stood there staring, guns pointed, like they expected something more to happen. The sergeant looked and shouted: 'HOLD YOUR FIRE!'

I knelt beside her. She was pale and started coughing. Everything was lulled, like the volume had been lowered. I put my hand behind her head and my knuckles scraped on the ground. Some of the cops still hadn't moved. I turned and shouted 'Call a fuckin ambulance!'

Her breathing was in short gasps. Time passed. I felt her slip away. Losing strength. And there was nothing I could do. Malone arrived, looked down, said: 'What the fuck?'

Then he pulled the shooter aside and got the details.

Her voice got hoarse. 'This is it, Charlie.'

She was staring at the sky and I thought of our first night in the playground, ideal and innocent. Things were getting outta my control and it was driving me crazy.

'Don't pass out on me, babe. I need ya here with me.'

Her breathing became heavy. Each intake catching like a rough asthmatic wheeze. She spoke again: 'It's freezing.' I kissed her on the forehead. 'Charlie?'

'Yeah?'

'Where are you?'

Malone came over, hands in his pockets, frowning. He asked one of the cops: 'Is there an ambulance on the way?'

They told him there was. I kissed her again and said: 'We're waitin for an ambulance...'

'Yeah, but...'

'It's ok...'

Malone said: 'She's delirious with the loss of blood.'

They all walked away, like they couldn't watch. Some of them consoled the killer in the corner. She was still and the strength fell out of her hand. Her breathing became deep and coarse and a gurgling noise came from somewhere inside her.

'El Niño?'

There was noise as the paramedics arrived. They'd already been on the way to deal with the shot cop. One of them took me under the arms, said: 'We'll have to ask you to move, sir.'

I stood back and watched them check her pulse. They put her on a stretcher and examined the wound. Took supplies from a bag. Dressed it as best they could and carried her off. I followed. Made eye contact with Malone. He attempted to say something but decided against it. On the way out, we passed the bodies of Anto, Simon and P.J — all either dead or dying.

Chapter Twenty-Five

The siren wailed. We took off. Interior. Ambulance. They worked fast. Had her on drips, masks and machines. One of the paramedics sat opposite me. Gave him mid-thirties, clean shave, well built. Piercing blue eyes, air of consideration meets professionalism. He had a clipboard in one hand, biro in the other, looking thoughtful. He opened. 'Are you the next of kin?'

'I guess so.'

'Brother? Cousin?'

'Boyfriend.'

'What's her name?'

'El Niño.'

He guessed the spelling. Wrote it down, said: 'I need to ask you some questions about her medical history. Sorry, what's *your* name?'

'Charlie.'

'Charlie, I'm Noel.' We shook hands. 'Charlie, are you aware of any medical conditions she might have?'

'No.'

'She smoke?'

'Yeah.'

'How many a day?'

'Twenty to thirty.'

He murmured as he wrote it down. 'Right, and is she on any medication — inhalers, painkillers, that kinda thing?'

'Never saw her take any.'

He scribbled some more. 'What about her home address? Her parents name?'

'Her folks are dead and I don't know where she lived before I met her.'

He looked, considered what he might say, but thought against it.

'That'll do for now, Charlie. Good man.'

'She gonna be ok?'

'I can't really say at the moment. She's suffered a lot, but she's got youth on her side.'

I didn't answer and he moved away. She was wrapped in a blanket and strapped into the stretcher. I could only see her closed eyes over the roof of the oxygen mask. Figured it was gonna be fine. As long as she was breathing, and surrounded by doctors, she'd be ok. I sat navigating the bumps and reading the directions on the side of the door. I heard the radio in the front squawk through. Another ambulance was looking for directions to Ballinrobe.

We got to the hospital. Noel took control. Wheeled her through. I followed. We were instantly surrounded by nurses, drips; injections. Calls for x-rays, operations, more oxygen; and morphine. I was pushed back and told to wait outside.

Couldn't sit. Went outside for a smoke. Felt like I was walking on air. Walked around the car park. Hands shaking, head spinning, stomach on fire. Knew there was one thing that could settle my nerves. Walked to the gate, saw The Traveller's Friend. Thought about it. Fought it and walked back.

Interior. Got a strong whiff of antiseptic. Hospitals. Got to the counter, said: 'I wanna enquire about a patient.'

'Name please?'

'El Niño?'

She looked up, said: 'That's it?'

'Yes.'

She asked me to spell it, then typed it in. It didn't come up. She asked: 'When was she admitted?'

'Bout half an hour ago.'

'Well then she wouldn't be registered yet, would she?'

I shrugged. She picked up the phone, dialled, listened. Left it down. 'She's in the operating theatre. You'll have news in about three hours.'

'Anythin else?'

'That's all I can say for now.'

Went for another smoke.

Feeling useless.

After, sat back in casualty and – don't ask how the fuck I did it – but I slept.

Woke up, hand on my shoulder, shadow over me. Neck creaked from the strain. This prick again. Malone. And he still hadn't gotten a haircut. 'How is she?'

'You don't care.'

'I wouldn't be here otherwise.'

'Unless you didn't catch Kramer.'

'He escaped, but we got the rest of them.'

'You want to know if I'll still testify.'

'I'm concerned about that kid. I feel partially responsible.'

'That's where you're wrong.

'What?'

'You're totally responsible.'

'My man said it was dark, there was a weapon. He couldn't be sure.'

'So he shot first?'

'They were warned of the potential dangers when they entered, and let's not forget, one of our own was injured too.'

'Yeah, they were real fuckin pros alright.'

'Kramer's more responsible than anyone.'

'This is the point where you ask me again: *will you still testify?*'

Pause. He asked. 'You hear anything from the doctors?'

'She's in surgery. It's gonna take a while before they know anythin.'

'The other three are here as well.'

'Great. Spark the champagne; let's have a reunion.'

'If she lives, I can guarantee you both immunity, and a safe life on the other side of the world. We've never been closer to nailing him.'

'I don't give a fuck if you send me to the moon. I'm finished with all this bullshit — you, Kramer, this whole fuckin circus.'

'Then her injuries are all for nothing.'

'They always were.'

'I'm trying to help you, Charlie.'

'You wanna help?'

'Yeah.'

'Then do me a favour.'

'Anything.'

'Fuck off!!'

He put his hands in his pockets, stared for a while, scratched his crotch and left.

The light was hurting my eyes. I leaned forward, put my head in my palms, felt like there was someone breaking rocks inside. Got up. Same cow behind the counter. Thought she'd recognise me but she hadn't a clue. I said: 'El Niño.'

'Excuse me?'

'I want to know about a patient by that name.'

She looked through some charts and typed it in. It was registered. Bent her head in closer, examined. Picked up the phone, got through, said: 'Hello, Mark, there's a gentleman here enquiring about a patient called *El Niño*?'

She bit her finger, said: 'Hmm...hm....yes...I see.' She hung up, said: 'Dr. McAndrew will be here to talk to you in a minute. You can take a seat while you wait.'

Sat with my hands in my pockets. Watching the television but unable to concentrate. There was a woman in the corner that couldn't stop coughing. Another hand on my shoulder. Looked up, young face. Stethoscope, clipboard. Air of authority, almost charisma.

'Are you Charlie?'

'Aye.'

'I'm Dr. McAndrew. I was in surgery with El Niño.'

I said nothing, let him continue. 'It's not good news, Charlie.'

'It was never gonna be.'

'Your girlfriend suffered some severe wounds to the abdomen and lung. We did everything we could, but...she didn't make it. I'm sorry.'

Times like that you expect something to happen, like an explosion. But it doesn't; and that's the deafening part. The world just keeps fuckin turning. I didn't believe a word of it, said: 'I wanna see her.'

He frowned. Thought about it and relented, said: 'Follow me.'

We walked down a long, white corridor. Reminded me of when I did the same thing for the old man.

Interior. Hospital morgue. El Niño on a bed, pale as a full moon. Doc said: 'Take as long as you like.'

There was no huge trauma, making her hard to recognise. It was unmistakably her but never more beautiful. I stood at the edge, leaning on the steel post, unsure of what to do. I touched her face; it was cold and her mouth was almost closed. There was a small glint of her teeth coming through. I leaned down and kissed her lightly. She tasted glossy, like stone, but with a faint taste of *her*.

She looked at peace, but I suppose all dead people do. The final sleep. She never became immortal, but she never got old. With a shock, I realised she wasn't coming back. This wasn't an illness, a temporary situation.

There was complete silence. When you're looking at a body like that, for long enough, you expect it to talk. It's like your brain wants to make it easier and convince you the person is still alive. I watched her face, expected a twitch, a smile, her to sit up and light a smoke.

I took her hand but didn't cry. I just held it and let its essence sink into my palm. She died more each second, like time was chipping away at all she was. I kissed her again – she tasted like candle wax – and left.

Met the doc on the way out. He slowed me up with concerned eyes. I stalled. Let him open, he said: 'I'm sorry...again.'

'It's not your fault.'

'That's not what I...'

Gave him a pat on the shoulder, said: 'I'll be in touch.'

Walked on and still felt his eyes. He called after me: 'You gonna be ok?'

'Me? Yeah, I'll be just fine.'

Exterior. Hospital entrance. Put a smoke in my mouth. It blew away with the wind. I whispered: *Cunt* and lit another.

Castlebar. Friday night. There was a stench of diesel. I was feeling cold, like I was built with indifference. Had a scatter of plans. They all involved lunacy, the calculated type. Took the exit. Got out onto the road. Taxis, cars and bikes flew past. All self-absorbed, in a hurry to private havens. No note of death, except on me. Drizzle started. A car pulled up beside me. Real kerb crawler shit, like a stalker. Gave him credit for persistence. The door flew open and I figured it was a lift home. Hopped in — he was like an eternal mannequin. Same suit, tie, moustache, hair that never moved. I pulled the door closed. He indicated, put on the wipers and said: 'Under normal circumstances, I wouldn't allow smoking in my car.'

'Time to adapt, Kojak. You're talkin super fuckin paranormal now.'

He revved hard and let the clutch come up too fast. The engine coughed and spluttered and cut out. We floated out onto the road and he hissed: *Bitch*. He turned the key and started it again. I almost went for the belt but apathy got the better of me, said: 'Good to know I'm in safe hands.'

He said nothing and pulled off like a granny, all slow and observation. Today FM on the radio, Tom Dunne's *Pet Sounds*, Interpol: *Take you on a Cruise*. Legendary stuff, it lasted ten seconds before he knocked it off and said: 'Shite.'

Tipped ash on ground, deliberation taking hold. I watched the white line, continuous then intermittent. He cracked at Ballintubber.

'I want to apologise again.'

I lit another smoke, the last one had been rubbed into the upholstery and crushed on the mat underneath. He continued, with exactly what I thought he'd continue with. 'You can help put him away for good, Charlie.'

'I know.'

'If not for yourself, then for the sake of her memory, and what she died for.'

'Aye.'

'It's a ticket out. You have everything to gain.'

'I'll do it, whatever the fuck you want me to do, I'll do it.'

He glanced over, then back at the road. 'You'll testify?'

'Yeah, fuck it.'

Could feel a million questions coming, but he held himself, like the moment was delicate.

'I want them all to go down, John. Life sentences, no parole, the works.'

He nearly crashed the fuckin car. Tried to keep his voice calm. 'That's...good, Charlie. We can work on that right away.'

He accelerated, went through Ballyheane and then Partry. He said: 'Everything's set up, ready to go. I have a list of places, once you chose where, we set the ball rolling and that's it.'

'Cool.'

'You'll have to point them out in court of course.'

Exhaled a circle of smoke, said: 'Absolutely.'

Felt like there was a shield between me and the world. Got to Ballinrobe. The cop station was on the right. He swung in hard and turned off the ignition, asked: 'Are you ready to go through what happened tonight?'

'Yeah.'

'Simon and P.J are still alive. They have some serious head wounds, but they'll recover. They were unconscious when we got to them. Anto's dead. We know that Kramer killed him, but you'll have to act as a witness.'

'Any word on his whereabouts?'

'He's still at large, but we have plenty of men on it.'

'That's fuckin professional. A dead, innocent girl, and an escaped drug dealin murderer. Ten outta ten, Malone. How'd you know where to find us anyway?'

'When you left here, we followed. Once my men heard the shot, they stormed in.'

'And you *still* fucked it all up.'

'He'll stick his head out again soon, just to let us know we haven't got the better of him.'

'He ain't that stupid.'

'But he *is* vain, and that's what we're banking on.'

'I'd have a plan B, just in case.'

'All the roads out of town are blocked. He's here somewhere. Maybe you know where he's gone?'

'Been out of his circle for years.'

'Think about it. Something might occur to you.'

'I'll check out a few haunts, ask a few questions. Somethin comes up, I'll give ya the tip.'

'That means letting you loose. Can I trust you?'

'I'm here of my own free will, you ain't lettin me do anythin, but if it settles your nerves, I'm not goin anywhere.'

'Meet me again in twenty-four hours?'

'Yeah. I'll call you.'

I left the door swinging open, just to piss him off. Pulled up my collars and walked. Something he said had clicked with me. I had a notion of where Kramer might be. Give it a name, call it gut instinct. Heard Malone switch on the car alarm with a squawk. The streetlamps on High Street gave the place an orange glow. I walked up the hill and let decisions make themselves. Solutions came through like moments of clarity, and all the time I felt a slow burning release.

I missed her beside me. The anticipation of her body. I expected her to be at the house when I arrived, but I was met with a roaring absence. It hit me like an artic truck at high speed. I walked through the rooms and our transparent memories. Everything still wrecked but her scent was in the air, mixed with something musty. I felt like I was searching, but didn't know what for; it just seemed like the right place to come. I got to our makeshift bedroom and lit a cigarette. Her spirit rode with me. I carried it like a jewel. Time to visit Kramer.

CHAPTER TWENTY-SIX

I walked down the Creagh Road, passed the holiday homes and through the dark woodland. It was raining and the trees rustled impatiently, dropping conkers and leaves in front of my feet. I kicked them ahead. Hands in my coat pockets, head down. Planning a dialogue, knowing he'd have one prepared.

The grass left a damp shadow on my shoes and I thought about the last time I'd been here. It looked conspicuous in the moonlight but hadn't changed much besides. Same colour, but surrounded by a lot of weeds that made it look decrepit. There was light, like from an oil lamp, inside. I got to the door and pulled it back by the latch. It came easy, damp like soft bread, ready to be broken. Creaked too, rusty hinges, Hitchcock style.

Interior. Safe house. Kramer sat at the old farmer's table. Looking smug,. Bottle of whiskey beside him. He said: 'Step into my parlour.'

His face was lit up by a candle on the table. 'Last person who said that to me ended up dead.'

'Probably deserved it too.'

Pause, I looked around. Found an old beer crate, said: 'Good thing you're not predictable.'

'I'm always one step ahead, Charlie. You took your time.'

I sat opposite him. He said: 'Back to where we started, eh?'

'It's over, Kramer.'

'It's never over.'

'Simon and P.J are goin down. Joe's talkin. They have the tapes and they got you nailed for killin Anto. There ain't no way out.'

'Fuck em all. I'll find a way.'

'Not this time.'

Silence, he took a swig. 'I never thought you'd sell out, Charlie. All this time, I figured you'd come round.'

'Two things: I ain't sold out, and I ain't ever gonna come round.'

'Then why you here?'

I said nothing. He frowned, took out a wrap of coke and cut it up. I smoked. He said: 'It's about the girl.'

'Hole in one.'

'Damn she was sweet.'

'Don't disrespect her.'

He sniggered, said: 'Bit late for that, Charles. What? She dead or somethin?'

Stayed quiet. He swigged, said: 'Shit, that's what all that shootin was. Heard it when I was gettin out. Thought it was all at me.'

'I'm holdin you responsible.'

'I wasn't even there.'

'You shouldn't've taken her. She had nothin to do with it.'

'Shit happens.'

'You fucked up.'

'Hey, Charlie, chill the fuckin beans. She was just a chick. I've had birds like her at three a night. Get over it.'

'That's where you're wrong.'

'Whatever, you wanna be a loved up pussy...go ahead. I don't fuckin care.'

He took a line. After, he swung back in his chair, hands in his pockets, looking confident, said: 'Charlie, we ain't here for the reminiscence, or to talk about dead dames. You didn't walk down here just to have a smoke.'

'You got that fuckin right.'

'Way I see it, only one of us can walk outta here alive.'

'I agree.'

'Let's put some honour into it.'

'What d'you know about honour?'

He took out a pistol, real Dirty Harry style, let it thump on the table. It hit the wood like a brick, thought the legs were gonna go. It was pointed right at me. For a second I expected a shot, like he was gonna shoot me right there.

'Russian Roulette.' His eyes were wide and psycho. 'I walk, you don't testify, one less rat I have to think about. You walk, you get revenge for your bitch, and do what the fuck you want, but that ain't gonna happen.'

'Why's that?'

'Because I'm fuckin invincible.'

'We'll see.'

He let the shells fall on the table. Tried to stare me out but I stayed deadpan. He took one up and slotted it in. Smoke rose between us. Darkness except for the wax. It was silent besides and I got a whiff of the whiskey. He rolled the barrel, it made the clicking sound you'd expect, like fingers across a comb. He left it down, said: 'Who first?'

'I'll do the honours.'

Took it in my hand. Deceptive weight. Looked shiny. Coarse handle on my palm. It gave me a sense of power. He said: 'Before you die, I want you to know that this is not the way I wanted things to turn out...it could have been a whole lot different...'

'You're full of shit.'

'I had big plans, Charlie. Big plans.'

'You're a selfish fuck.'

'I woulda brought you all the way to the top.'

'I didn't want it.'

'Everybody wants it. Just some cunts think it's noble to deny it.'

'Greed?'

'Power.'

'Yeah, powerful shit, Kramer. Hangin out in an outhouse, hidin from the fuzz — my fuckin hero, Kramer.'

He looked at the pistol. I put it to my temple. Heart jumped a beat, sweat came through. Pulled the trigger. Heard the click, like a pen hitting the ground. Chamber empty. I unhooked the barrel and spun it, slid it across the table. He said: 'At least there'll be some competition.' Pushed the wrapper my way. 'Want a line while before you die?' I said nothing. He picked up the bottle. 'How bout a swig of the demon?'

Had a mock temptation. He laughed with wheezy, loud echoes. Put the gun to his head and said: 'Balls of fuckin steel, Charlie. Balls of fuckin steel!'

Pulled it, click. He banged the pistol on the table, said: 'I am a fuckin animal!'

He shoved the gun towards me. Then started on another line. I took it up and he leaned back, rubbing his nose. Obviously fuckin invigorated, said: 'You know, Charlie, back in the old days, you were slick, had style. You were a tough nugget, even when you were drunk. I'm gonna miss ya when you blow your fuckin head off.'

I went slow this time. Let it rest for a second, looked him in the eyes and pressed. Thought I saw discomfort, like he was surprised when it didn't fire. I slid the piece over. He inspected it, as if it were an artefact, then said: 'Glad that didn't go, man. I almost forgot to tell you what a fun time we had with your girl.'

Hands itching to attack, I said: 'Shut up and shoot.'

'Dames like her are dangerous, ya know. Off the wall, drive a guy crazy. I think she made you soft, man. She was a good ride, though. Not too tight, but better than most hookers, you know?' He looked right at me. 'You know, I think she liked it, in a fucked up, sick kinda way, I think she even wanted more...'

'I don't believe a fuckin word outta your coked up, fucked up mouth.'

'Yeah you do, even if you don't wanna. You know I'm sayin the truth.'

I said nothing. Things went quiet. He was still inspecting the gun, I asked: 'Scared?'

'That word ain't even in my vocabulary.'

He put the weapon in his mouth, shoved it back real hard and pulled the trigger.

Click.

He started laughing again, real loud, pushed the gun over and said: 'It's damn tough bein this good.'

I spun the barrel. He lit a smoke. The place was colder than ever, adrenaline thick in the air. Expected him to gnaw at me some more. Took my time, I was feeling real Kamikaze, like I'd nothing to lose. He was trying to play it cool but I could tell he was getting impatient.

There was a film of sweat on the handle and the barrel dug into my cheek, putting pressure on my gum. My finger slid on the trigger and the inner mechanics amplified in my ear. Each centimetre made his head churn, stressing him out. He took a long draught of whiskey, said: 'Just fuckin die, will ya?'

Click.

Nothing.

He drank long and deep again, went: 'You're a real piece of work, Charlie. Pity you couldn't keep that whore alive too.'

'Watch your mouth.'

'She was a slut, and she loved it, took it everywhere — mouth, ass, cunt. Coulda given it to her in the eyes — she'd have let us too. Oh yeah, have I said that? We all had her. Me, Simon, P.J and even Anto, the ugly fuck.'

Handed him the gun, said: 'You might need this.'

'And yeah, she liked the taste of cum too, especially mixed. Two, three guys, all blowin the load in her face.'

'Careful, Kramer, I'm fuckin tellin ya.'

'And she screamed, oh yeah, how she screamed, she fuckin wailed your name all over The Bowers.' He put his voice to a high pitch. 'Charlie, Charlie, Charlie, but Charlie wasn't around. He was up takin it from Malone, gettin rode like a fuckin rodeo. So we had to oblige…'

He took up the gun. Played casual. Took his turn. Click. Threw it back at me. Kept going. 'And then she went unconscious, which was better, coz we didn't have to listen to her shit. And we just kept goin and goin and goin.' He patted his pockets, like he was looking for something. 'She muttered a few times too, like when we'd be switchin shifts and that. I always took the longest, coz I wanted her to enjoy it, ya know? And then we were all tryin to do her together and…'

The crack was loud, violent, and involved blood. Lots of it. Thought the walls were gonna blow away. In better times, two blanks was enough time for Kramer to tear a man apart, but now he was fat and slow. It hit him in the side of the neck. He tried to jump out of the chair but fell back against the wall. He covered the wound with his hand and tried to catch his breath in gasps and coughs. I flipped the table over, expecting a fright, or horror at my action. None came. He attempted to talk but could only make choking sounds. Then he collapsed, face down.

Carefully, I took the bullets from the ground and loaded them with steady hands. Blood oozed onto the floor and the remnants of his last fix of cocaine were scattered beside him. He lay panting like a vicious, dying animal. I rolled him round, took aim, looked him in the eye and shot him twice in the head. His body jolted and went limp and his leg twitched for a second, then went dead and the silence roared.

They say your pose in death is a reflection of how you lived your life. His eyes were open. Displaying defiance, like something heavy was about to fall on his head. I gave him two kicks to the face and a couple more in the stomach. Then I lit a smoke, took the whiskey and poured some over him. Splashed the rest of the bottle around the walls and floor. After, I threw the cigarette on his corpse and the flames were up in seconds.

Exterior. Outside the hut. The gun was heavy in my waist as I walked, leaving the crack and sizzle of the fire behind.

Exit Kramer.

Chapter Twenty-Seven

I was the only one at the funeral. No one else there that mattered. The hospital left the whole thing to me. I had the choice of getting the state to pay, but fuck that.

Got the local undertaker in Ballinrobe. Thin man, lotsa patience. Looked like Pete Postlewaithe. Asked me where it would *leave* from. I gave him hints on the condition of my house. He frowned and said we could use the hospital. He went down that night and did what undertakers do — prepared her for the service and the crowds that wouldn't show.

The next day. He drove the hearse to Castlebar. The doctor – McAndrew - saw me coming but didn't say much. He acknowledged Pete. They were familiar. We walked to the morgue in silence. The place was cold and smelled of formaldehyde. I spotted her immediately, saw her pale face coming over the rim of the open coffin. After a respectful silence, the two men blessed themselves and I gave the nod to close the lid. I looked away as they covered her for the last time, knowing the image would haunt me til the end of my days.

Me and Pete wheeled her out and the doc pulled me aside as we reached the entrance. 'You ok?'

'Yeah, sure doc. Cheers.'

Extended his hand, said: 'Take care of yourself.'

We had a strong handshake and I said: 'Will do.'

We drove out. Slow and with respect. People on the path blessed themselves as we passed. I checked out the wing mirror, saw McAndrew standing at the door, watching us leave, hands in his coat pockets. He went outta view as we turned on to the main road.

Exit Castlebar. Radio silence all the way home. Got to the church in Ballinrobe in time for 10 o'clock mass. Low key affair, small attendance. Pete had the priest sorted with the situation and the mass was dedicated to El Niño. He was efficient, but not without compassion. After, he did the ritual — incense, holy water, incantations, all that.

Exterior. Outside the church. Rain. Believers standing around, watching, asking, wondering. Some of them had their hands clasped and their heads down. A few men stood by the door, smoking, chatting, laughing. They hushed when they saw us.

The bells kicked in overhead as we wheeled her to the hearse. There were no roses or tributes and the back door was open like a gate into the afterlife. Pete and I pushed on as the rain got worse. I had my right hand on the golden handle and my left on the back, rolling her along. Some Neil Young lyrics were strong on my mind: 'You are just a dreamer, but I am just a dream.' The priest followed, waving his magic lamp and a mobile phone squealed somewhere in the sparse audience.

Folks slipped away as we sat in and faced for the cemetery.

—

The plot was in Ballinrobe graveyard, parallel to the Church View estate. Folks there were born astride a grave. I spent the night before digging. Pete had had two punters organised, but I turned them down. I took their shovels and set to work.

It was our family plot. The last thing the old man did was make sure we all had a final bed. It took me til morning to dig the full six feet. I had only the whispers of the dead for company. Afterwards, I sat on the mound, having a smoke and watching the sunrise. My clothes and face were layered in clay and my hands were blistered, but I welcomed the warm feel of physical work in my blood. I looked down into the blankness of the open grave and had waves and sight distortions. There was no chill or fear, only a sense of certainty.

Dawn comes early with rosy fingers. When she came, I stubbed out my smoke and took in the smell of grass, the sound of birds and life and the hum of newly awoken engines in the distance. Then I walked to the gate and home, accompanied on either side by the past, the present and the future.

—

Swung in with Pete. The collar was waiting, bible in his hand. Didn't seem phased, all in a day's work. He said the piece, did a decade of the Rosary and we lowered her. The whole thing was like a charade made for reality TV. He threw in the clay – ashes to ashes – and said: 'It's not the manner in which we die that is important; it's how we are remembered.'

Pete nodded, more prayers followed. After, the Priest asked me if I wanted to be on my own. Cos there was nothing more they could do. I said ok. They left.

I stood there alone for a while. All my anger was harnessed in bitterness and rage, built on a bed of resolve. Then it was time. The first throw of clay hit the lid hard and fell off. The next one did the same. Soon enough the box had disappeared. It was late afternoon when I'd finished and the grave bulged beside me. I threw the shovel aside and let the wind run through me wild. Neil Young's solo playing on my nerves, like the pain of dying memories. More rain. It was time to go.

CHAPTER TWENTY-EIGHT

The rain got worse. I lit a smoke, the end got wet, but it still sparked. I inhaled hard and my lungs squealed. It felt good. Pete's house was on Church Lane, between Cummins' car park and the tip of New Street.

The door was silver, stained-glass window, bad letterbox with furry shit around the edges. Knocked, no answer. Knocked again and it creaked open. Pete's head appeared with confused, squinted eyes. Day traffic slushed behind me. 'Charlie?'

'Well.'

'Is anything wrong?'

'It's all good. Just wanna fix up the bill.'

'What? But, it's so soon. I still need to write it up.'

I shrugged, said: 'So write it. I'll wait.'

'Today?' He looked at his watch, pulled the door back and said: 'Step in for a minute.'

Interior. Pete's place. Hallway. Green walls, plush carpet. There was a smell of car freshener. Stuffed pheasant on the wall. It looked shocked and fat. Portrait of a horse beside it. Pete scuttled into a room on the left. There was almost silence but something ticked in the belly of the house and the cars could be heard outside. Could hear him shuffling. Then he walked through, without any acknowledgement, into another room.

Hallstand beside me. Had a mirror. Coat and hat hanging. Umbrella underneath. Phone on the tabletop. Old model, looked awkward and heavy. Green, with one of those round dials, the ones you have to twist round every time you want a digit. Rosary beads left beside it and a picture of some holy woman.

Took a shot at my reflection. I looked haggard and drawn, sunken eyes. Turned and saw the edge of the kitchen, tiled floor. Heard the sound of ripping paper. Biro hitting the tablecloth and the chair getting pushed back. Pete arrived, piece of paper in his hand, said: 'Now, here it is.'

He walked into the kitchen and tried to occupy himself. I took a glance, pulled out my wad and rolled off the notes. He came back, asked: 'Would you like tea?'

'No thanks, Chief. Kind of in a hurry.'

Handed him the grade. He took it without looking and said: 'I was sorry for your trouble.'

'You did a good job.'

The phone rang, loud and angry, like a fire alarm. I made to leave. He said: 'I better get this.'

'I gotta go anyway. I'll see ya round.'

'I hope not.'

Exterior. Church Lane. Pulled up my collar. The residue of the house rested in the back of my throat and my bones ached against the cold. Next step of the plan was to make a call. Walked down High Street. Passed a joint called Mooney's. On down to the bottom of the hill. Took a left at the trees, fallen leaves flushing through my feet. Went up the steps and got to the point where I'd first met Kramer. Took out my phone and dialled. Malone answered right away.

'Charlie? Where the hell've you been?'

'I had a funeral.'

Instrumental, then: 'Where are you now?'

'In The Bowers.'

'The situation's changed.'

'How?'

'Kramer's dead. We found his body yesterday.'

'I heard.'

He was silent again, I said: 'So what now?'

I imagined him having a shrug. 'He's out of the picture. That's the important thing.'

'I don't think so.'

'Why not?'

'Nature abhors a vacuum.'

'What's that supposed to mean?'

'It's only a matter of time before someone fills the slot.'

'You think someone's ready to move in straight away?'

'Yeah, first Max made things organised, then Kramer came and took him on, and now someone's gotta come next.'

Pause. He asked: 'Who?'

'I'm not at liberty to discuss that information.'

'The line's safe.'

'I prefer face to face.'

'Call up to the station.'

'It's too risky. I'm bein watched.'

'Where, then?'

'Call down here.'

'The Bowers?'

'Alone. I don't want the fuckin cavalry.'

Sigh, then: 'What part are you in?'

'On the bridge.'

He thought for a second, clicked his tongue, said: 'Give me about ten minutes.'

I sat on the ledge and waited amidst more ghosts of the past. Memories of the old days. The drinking and the buzz of the robbing. The rain came down hard and I stood up and paced. The tips of my ears were cold. I checked out my phone, scrolled through the old text messages, all from her. Thought about reading them, then deleted them all.

Heard the gravel crunch under his wheels. I walked to the bridge, rested my hands on the edge, smoked and watched. He got out, looked around and tucked his shirt inside his pants. Some birds flew from the embankment beside him. I tipped my brow like a sailor but he gave no acknowledgment, just walked in my direction. I watched the river while I waited. Brown flow with white flecks like spit and the silhouette of an old rusted bicycle beneath. He came into my peripheral vision and I didn't stir. He stood beside me, lit a cigarette and said: 'Well?'

I said nothing. He continued: 'I've put a lot of time into you, Charlie, and got very little back. This better be good.'

'Believe me it is.'

'Well...let's have it.'

Threw my smoke in the water and asked: 'You like your job, Malone?'

'It has its moments.'

'What's your favourite part?'

'Putting criminals away, long term. What's your point?'

'What d'ya think about the thing with Kramer?'

'His death, or his legacy?'

'Him being smoked?'

'Relieved, and a little robbed.'

'Robbed?"

'Relief because it's one less thug on the streets. Robbed because I didn't get to nail him. Do you know who's responsible?'

'He pissed the wrong people off.'

'You think it might've been a turf thing?'

'No.'

He looked into the distance, flicked his smoke away and said: 'Gimme your theory, Charlie. It's cold out here, and I want put a lid on this...enough games.'

'I killed Kramer.'

He was genuinely surprised, said: 'What?'

'You heard me.'

'You?'

'Yeah.'

'Why?'

'You're not a very good detective, are you?'

The cogs turned, he said: 'The girl?'

'The girl.'

'Jesus.'

I figured he was assessing the consequences, playing with his conscience. He said: 'It's *almost* understandable.'

'I think it makes perfect sense.'

'Not in the eyes of the law.'

'Fuck the law. A tooth for a tooth.'

'Two wrongs don't make a right.'

'They do in my book.'

'Well you don't respect the fabric of society.'

'It's all relative.'

'You've just admitted murder to a detective. You can't expect me to turn a blind eye to that?'

'Even though it relieved you?'

'My bias doesn't matter. The law knows no prejudice.'

'But you do.'

'I know my job. That's what counts.'

'You don't know a fuckin thing.'

We were silent. He took out his cuffs, said: 'It's nothing personal, Charlie. It never was.'

'It's always personal, Malone, and I'm not finished with gettin my own justice.'

He was incredulous, said: 'I think you are.'

'You're no different. You think you are, but you're just as much a criminal as any of us.'

'I have the greater good in mind.'

'You lost your way. Makin deals and playin people.'

'It's a war, Charlie, and like I keep saying, every war's got casualties, even innocent people, like…that girl.'

'El Niño.'

'It doesn't matter. The fact is, you can't just murder people because you're pissed off.'

'I beg to differ.'

'I think I'm wasting my time.'

'It's over, John.'

'It sure is. You're under arrest.'

He reached inside again, figured he was going for his gun, but I had the speed. I took out the piece and pointed. It spelled currency. He tried to play it cool, like he was in control.

'What's with the gun, Charlie?'

'It's a war, Malone. People die. Every war's got casualties.'

'Get a grip, kid. You're adding years to your sentence by the second.'

'Life is life for me, chief, inside or out. Hell is a state of mind.'

'You haven't got the balls.'

'We'll see.'

I cocked the hammer. It gave him a kick. He tried reason, said: 'Charlie…put the weapon down. You're making a huge mistake. We can settle this another way.'

'You're a soldier, I'm a soldier.'

'Look, I'm sorry about your girlfriend, ok? I'm really sorry, but there was nothing that could be done.'

'Falls a bit short, John.'

'Don't do this, there are options...'

'Like jail?'

'Like... something, just calm down.'

'Fraid I'm past the point of calm.'

He tried a different approach, said: 'I have officers all around here, watching this whole exchange.'

'Nice try.'

'You won't make it to the top of the hill.'

'But you'll be long dead by then.'

'I got a family.'

'I'll send them your regards.'

Enter anger, he said: 'You fuckin scumbag.'

'You fucked up.'

'You'll go down for this, Charlie.'

'Give it a name. Any last words?'

'What do you expect me to say?'

'You're a detective. Detect this.'

The first shot hit him on the nose and made a mess of his face. I followed in quick succession with a second. He fell back, gurgled a bit and died.

I stood over him and watched his life dissipate, then gave him another one in the temple, just to make sure. He was splayed like a scarecrow. Carrion for the vultures. Had a shake in my hand from the rounds, but I felt otherwise collected. I threw the gun over the bridge and walked back into the town's oblivious existence.

Chapter Twenty-Nine

I was back in Galway that evening. Had plans forming, like notions about skipping the country, but knew I'd get hung with the passport. Got a hostel off Woodquay. Modern gig, lotsa backpackers and activity, easy to stay anonymous.

They have televisions in each room and leave folks to themselves. A couple of evenings ago I clocked a picture of myself on the box. It was a bad snap from the time I dropped the agent. I looked drunk and depressed. At least I was harder to recognise and it cut me some slack in public.

I see her everywhere now. Across the street, behind a delivery van, the back of her head disappearing into a shop. Her voice calls my name from a distance. I see her in my reflection, her spirit hovering around me. All the time I hear about storms and weather phenomena. Get her scent from people passing, hear stories about London and other places to travel. My mind picks up on all this shit. Like a radar, it hones in. Tunes from Mike Oldfield, Moby, Neil Young, all sending out her echoes.

The nights are cold and long and bring demons for company. The future stays dark and numb, offering nothing. I figure I'm not even living, just a ghost of myself. All the time I'm watching newspapers, TV, even people's eyes, for signs of my guilt.

I spend a lot of time on the streets, head down, kicking stones and dodging the cracks, looking for a distraction. Nothing comes. The city is awash with students and innocence. Thoughts swirl and corruption hovers around my mind, always looking for a chink.

The room is dark tonight with the only light coming from the television. Its muted screen shows pictures of war. The table in front of me is strewn with old papers, filthy plates and cigarette skins. Outside, I can hear the swish of the cars go by on the quiet winter road. Particles of dust float through the TV's spectrum. There's a party below and I can hear the muffled laughter and the intermittent strumming of an acoustic guitar. Bottles clunk together and people run up and down the stairs. I'm thinking about a walk, but there's nowhere to go. I could try sleep, but I know it won't come. There's a movie on later, but I know I won't concentrate. I want to stay in, but it'll drive me crazy.

I want to join them downstairs, although I'll have nothing to say. I could go out and rob, but it's too risky. Everything I do is loud. A cup falls into the sink and it rattles my nerves. In the bathroom, I turn on a tap and it sounds like amplified radio static, scraping along my nerves. My reflection disgusts me. It's like a bad portrait of someone else. I don't know who this person is. My hands are shaking and my legs are weak, like I'm delirious or sick. There are goose pimples on my neck and from somewhere inside I can hear a slow throbbing vibration.

Back on the bed, I try tunes but they don't work. I can't sit still. I stand up, light a smoke and look around. My jacket's hanging on the hallstand by the door and my shadow dances behind it.

Exit Charlie.

Interior. Neachtains. Night. They say you take up where you left off. Some things about a pub are universal. Barman drying a glass, old guy in the corner, fire on. The place is dark brown. I give the heads up and he leaves down the towel. Hands in the back pocket, all enthusiastic. I give him my order, it comes, I pay and get the change. I let it sit. My bad picture's being broadcast in the corner. It's got volume, so you can hear it too. I lift the beverage and swirl, take in its aroma. I get a beer mat and put it underneath. I leave it back down and tap my knee. Not many in. Guy my age in the corner, sitting on his own, pint of Bud and an I-Pod. The reporter says my name and they show pictures of Ballinrobe. The fire, the crime scene at The Bowers. My house. Old pictures of Kramer too. Expressed sorrow at the loss of a fine detective. Talk of dealers and gangland turf wars and the recent death of a young woman.

The place is getting warm. I slide my fingers round the rim of the glass. The chair has arms designed for the elbows. I sit back and get cosy and let a rabid desire take hold.

Her name was El Niño, her father called her that because on the night she was born there was a storm. He said it signified the way she was to live her life. I raise my drink and salute the old man. He returns it. We drink in unison, me with less patience. It goes down fast, acidic and hard, and the breeze rustles across the back of my neck as a door slams behind me forever.

ACKNOWLEDGEMENTS

Special thanks are due to - Michelle Henson, Jonathan Williams, Shauna Kelly, Mike McCormack (and all the crew at the M.A. in Writing Class (2004)). Imelda Heaphy, Noel Duffy, Aine Tierney, Julia Wallis Martin, Lisa Martina Moran, Anna and Sean O'Maille, Pauline and Paddy Donnellan, Vinnie from Charlie Byrnes. Tom Page (Jack Hammer Publishing), Rick, Alex and all the Adams family at Orange City, Florida. Tom Fringe, Johnny Molloy, Eucharia Commins, Conor Kenny. Alan, Jody and Sam (Urban Pie Newspaper, Vancouver) The Stinging Fly, Fish Publishing, Kevin Higgins, The Galway Advertiser, The Connaught Tribune, The Mayo News, The Western People, The Galway Independent, The Celtic Connection, Vancouver. Kev, Pat and Martina Donnellan. The Galway Arts Centre. Mike Diskin, Joan Higgins (and all the staff at the Town Hall, Galway). Róisín Stack, Eamon Stack, Aindrias Stack, Eddie Stack, Liam Horan, The Langans and The Valkenburg, Joyce Laffey, Ballinrobe Community School, Mary Farragher (and all the staff at the Ballinrobe Library) Martin Murphy's Newsagent, Ballinrobe, Mary Jackson (and all the crew at the Family Resource Centre, Ballinrobe), Annie Chambers and Lenny, the Henson Family, and everyone involved at Truman Town Theatre. Thank you all for your invaluable support over the years. Special thanks to Seona Tully for modelling for the cover photo.